The Guest Cat

The Guest Cat

•

TAKASHI HIRAIDE

Translated by Eric Selland

A NEW DIRECTIONS PAPERBOOK ORIGINAL

Originally published as *Neko no Kyaku* by Kawade Shobo Shinsha, Tokyo, Japan. Published by arrangement with the author.

Manufactured in the United States of America
New Directions Books are printed on acid-free paper.
First published as a New Directions Paperbook Original (NDP1274) in 2014
Design by Erik Rieselbach

Library of Congress Cataloging-in-Publication Data
Hiraide, Takashi, 1950–
[Neko no Kyaku. English]
The Guest Cat / Takahashi Hiraide ; translated by Eric Selland.
pages cm
"A New Directions Book."
ISBN 978-0-8112-2150-4 (acid-free paper)
I. Selland, Eric, translator. II. Title.
PL852.I663N413 2014
895.63'5—dc23
                    2013046516

10 9 8 7 6 5 4

New Directions Books are published for James Laughlin
by New Directions Publishing Corporation
80 Eighth Avenue, New York 10011

THE GUEST CAT

1

AT FIRST IT LOOKED LIKE LOW-LYING RIBBONS OF clouds just floating there, but then the clouds would be blown a little bit to the right and next to the left.

The small window in the corner of our kitchen bordered on a tall wooden fence, so close a person could barely pass by. From inside the house, its frosted glass looked like a dim movie screen. There was a small knothole in the wooden fence and the green of the bamboo hedge—which was about ten feet wide, to the north of the alley—was always projected on to the crude screen. Whenever someone walked by in the narrow alleyway, a figure formed, filling the entire window. Viewed from the dark interior of the house, sunny days seemed ever more vivid, and working perhaps on the same principle as a camera obscura, the figures of people walking past were turned upside down. Not only that, but whatever images passed by came from the opposite direction than the one in which the people were actually walking. And as the passersby approached closer to the knothole, their over-turned figures would swell so large that they would entirely fill the window frame and, once they had passed, would suddenly disappear like some special optical phenomenon.

But on that day, the image of the ribbon clouds did not attempt to move past, and the image did not grow very large when it neared the knothole. Even when it should have expanded to an enlarged size, the image floating in the upper part of the window was only big enough to sit on the palm of one's hand. The ribbon clouds hesitated, as if hovering in the street, and then the sound of a feeble cry arose.

My wife and I had decided on a name for the little alleyway. We called it "Lightning Alley." It was about twenty minutes from the teeming Shinjuku terminal on a private line heading southwest: you got off at a little station where the express didn't stop and walked south for about ten minutes. There you hit a bit of an incline, and then at the top of the hill you crossed the only street with any significant traffic going east and west. Once you crossed that diagonally, the rest of the way was downhill, and after about a hundred yards down a wide, rambling incline, there was a house on the left with an old-fashioned fence, its bamboo slats attached vertically all along the bottom half of the plastered wall. Just before reaching its gate you turned in to the austere little alleyway on the left, while the road continued on along the wooden fence.

Located within these same plastered walls and wooden fence, on the extensive grounds of an old estate, the place we were renting had originally been a guesthouse. A little more than halfway down the alley, a rickety gate in the wooden fence doubled as the landlady's side entrance and the tenants' front gate. Like an eye that went unnoticed, the knothole was located just beyond that gate.

Passing by behind the fence without knowing just how plainly your image was being projected on our window, you would first run head-on into the brick wall of the house jutting out from the left, and then you would turn to the right at an acute angle. And just as suddenly you would run into a house whose roof was concealed behind the dense growth of a huge zelkova tree, at which point the path turned sharply again to the left. The frequent, sharp turns created the lightning-bolt pattern one often sees in drawings, so we jokingly referred to it as "Lightning Alley."

The zelkova tree shading the alley was of an advanced age. Quite likely the local district had designated it a protected tree. When the house had been built, it had been designed to provide an enclosure for the trunk of the tree. Its branches, which had been allowed to grow and spread unhindered, extended their luxuriant fingers from the east side of the landlady's garden, to over the northeastern corner where the tenants' cottage stood, providing all with the blessing of its leafy protection. By late autumn the yard would grow thick with fallen leaves, causing the landlady to heave many deep sighs.

It was a boy of around five from the house next door, also embraced by the great zelkova tree, who became determined to capture and keep the stray cat several days after it had first crept into Lightning Alley. Though they were our neighbors to the east, the twists and turns of Lightning Alley produced a distance between us. Despite our daily comings and goings, there was never an opportunity for us to meet face to face. The side of the neighbor's house bordering our garden was a solid wall with just one small window for ventilation. And to be blunt, we were simply renters of the guesthouse tucked back in a small corner of the extensive grounds of the estate, so there was little sense of our actually being true neighbors.

The boy often played where the alleyway turned sharply, shouting energetically in a high-pitched voice, but since our daily lives took place in such completely different time zones (mine spent facing a desk till late in the night) we rarely crossed paths. Even so, a voice recognizably his traveled over the fence, reaching me late one morning at the breakfast table and firmly announcing the intention to keep the cat.

A few days later, I noticed the cat scurrying around our garden—no more than the size required for hanging clothes out to dry—and then I heard the boy's voice and found myself breaking into a smile. Looking back now, I see this was a missed opportunity.

2

THE LITTLE BOY'S TRIUMPHANT PROCLAMATION MUST have been heard by the landlady inside the big house, for that evening we heard her talking in front of the neighbor's gate— "How'd you like to have a cat?"

The woman's dry voice was pressing. "It's just really too much for us," the voice went on, chatting blithely about how cats infiltrated the premises from every corner, laying waste to the garden, raising a racket on the roof, and sometimes even leaving muddy paw prints inside the house.

The young housewife next door spoke in a voice both quiet and refined. One would think she would have been placed on the defensive, but after patiently listening to the eighty-year-old's pleas, it appeared she had no trouble holding her own. In all likelihood she could see the boy standing behind his grandmother and assumed he was praying for dear life. And in the end, it seems it was the old woman who lost out.

I remembered that just two years earlier when we'd signed the lease to rent the guesthouse from the old woman, there was a clause appended to the agreement stating that no children or pets were allowed. Neither of us especially wanted a child at that point in our lives, even though we were on the verge of pass-ing beyond our mid-thirties. And when it came to what are re-ferred to as pets, neither of us especially liked cats, and the no-tion of owning a dog had never even come up. So you could say that based on the old woman's terms of occupancy, we were ex-tremely well-suited renters.

There are a few cat lovers among my close friends, and I have to admit that there have been moments when that look of exces-sive sweet affection oozing from around their eyes has left me feeling absolutely disgusted. Having devoted themselves to cats body and soul, they seemed at times utterly indifferent to shame. When I think about it now, rather than my not being a cat lover, it may simply have been that I felt a disconnect with people who were cat lovers. But more than anything, I'd simply never expe-rienced having one around.

I had a dog once when I was a child. I felt my relationship with the dog was simple and frank. The tension felt through the leash between the one who obeys and the one who leads was refreshing.

I must have been right around the same age as the little neigh-bor boy when I was living with my family in a row house which acted as a residence for municipal workers, though the row houses looked more like tenements in a slum than public build-ings. I had only just recently gotten the dog when somebody up and stole it. Most likely it was midafternoon on a Saturday or Sunday when my father noticed that the spitz, which had been tied up outside in front of the entry, was gone. "Dognappers ..." he grumbled, then immediately began trying to counteract the event. He stormed out of the house, taking me along, and we raced around in every direction in search of the spitz, but there was no sign of either dog or dognapper.

I remember clearly feeling that I shouldn't ask my father anything more about what had happened, seeing how he'd reacted when the dog went missing. My older sister insists I cried all night long, but I have no memory of that.

Although I myself did not especially like cats, my wife has an innate connection with all living things. From the time she was small, she would go out with her older brother to catch crawdads and salamanders and keep them in an aquarium. She says she even hatched butterflies of all kinds—they would fly around her room. She'd kept various kinds of birds, finches and canaries, and had also raised chicks. She'd cared for baby birds that had fallen out of the nest as well and even nursed wounded bats back to health.

Even now she would turn on the TV to a nature program and could correctly name all of the animals, even rare species in faraway countries. In my wife's case, what I mean by not liking cats is something of an entirely different order than her husband's attitude, since all her life she had engaged with a variety of animals with the same level of interest. So in other words, she did not have my sort of preference of dogs over cats.

Once the cat had become the next door neighbor's pet, it would often appear in the garden in a new vermilion collar, hung with a tinkling bell.

A simple wooden fence separated the yard of the main house and the little garden adjacent to the guesthouse—the two having originally been one. With its landscape of trees and little hills, pond and flower beds, the imposing garden of the main house was most agreeable to the cat. After first stepping into the guesthouse's small garden, the cat would set out on its own for the expanse of the big house's yard.

Whenever the door to our small garden was left open, the cat was in the habit of peeking inside our house on its way to and from the main yard. The cat wasn't a bit scared of humans. But it was cautious—just a natural part of its behavior perhaps—and would gaze at us quietly with its tail standing straight in the air, yet it would never come inside. If we tried to pick it up outside, it would quickly run away, and if we tried to force it to let us hold it, it would bite. Aware of the ever vigilant eye of the landlady, we made no real attempts to tame the cat.

These events unfolded between the autumn of 1988 and the beginning of winter, during the final months of the Shōwa Period.

3

THE CAT'S NAME WAS CHIBI, WHICH MEANS "LITTLE one." We could hear the boy's particularly high-pitched voice calling the cat: "Chibi!" Then we'd hear the sound of the boy's shoes running around outside, followed by the tinkling of the little bell announcing the cat's arrival.

Chibi was a jewel of a cat. Her pure white fur was mottled with several lampblack blotches containing just a bit of light brown. The sort of cat you might see just about anywhere in Japan, except she was especially slim and tiny.

These were her individual characteristics — slim and small, with ears that stood out, tapering off beautifully at the tips, and often twitching. She would approach silently and undetected to rub up against one's legs. At first I thought Chibi avoided me because I was not used to cats, but this seems not to have been the case. When a girl who often passed along Lightning Alley stopped and crouched to gaze at the cat, it did not run away. But as soon as she attempted to touch it, the cat quickly slipped off, avoiding contact at all costs. The cat's manner of rejection was like cold, white light.

Moreover, the cat rarely made a sound. As far as I remember, when it first appeared in the alley it made some sort of sound, but since then it had never let out a meow. It looked as if no matter how much time passed the cat was not going to let us hear its voice. This seemed to be the message the cat was giving us.

Another one of Chibi's characteristics was that she changed the direction of her cautious attention frequently. This active behavior wasn't limited to her kittenhood. Perhaps because she played alone most of the time in the expansive garden, she reacted strongly to insects and reptiles. And there were times when I could only conclude that she must be reacting to subtle changes in the wind and light, not detectable by humans. It may be that most cats share the same quickness, but even so, in Chibi's case, it was acute—she was, after all, the cat of Lightning Alley. My wife got into the habit of pointing to the cat whenever it went by, extolling its virtues.

Trained by the boy next door, Chibi had become quite skilled at playing with a ball. It seemed that the boy was using a rubber ball that fit right into the palm of one's hand. Sounds of laughter and play in the alley, and the regular bouncing of the ball, elicited such pleasant feelings that gradually I began to feel like trying it out for myself, here in our little garden. Finally one day, after a period of self-reflection, I took an old Ping-Pong ball—which had been shut away in the corner of a drawer—in my hand and headed for the garden.

I tried bouncing the Ping-Pong ball on the concrete below the open veranda. Chibi crouched, her eyes locked on the ball's movement. Then she lowered her entire body and became tense—with all four legs aligned as she gently lowered her haunches, contracting them so that they became slightly rounded like a cocked spring. From that position she leapt off the earth with a violent force, boldly pouncing on the small white ball. Then she batted the ball back and forth several times in mid-air between her two front paws, and next shot quickly through my legs and ran off.

Chibi's independence would manifest itself in unexpected ways, even while performing acts of incredible athletic skill. Casting aside the Ping-Pong ball, she turned about at an acute angle, yet in the next moment she had placed her tiny paw on the head of a toad concealed in the shade of one of the land-scape rocks. Then just as suddenly she flew to the other side of the garden, extending one of her front legs to slip into a clump of bushes. Next, showing her white belly, she looked in my direc-tion, twitching slightly. But there was no stopping there—with-out a glance at her human playmate, she leaped up and grabbed the sleeve of an undershirt swinging gently back and forth on the clothesline, then flashing through the wooden gate, she quickly retreated to the yard of the big house.

I had heard from one of my cat-lover friends that playing with a ball was something that cats only did when they are still kit-tens. But it seemed that Chibi, reaching adulthood, only picked up momentum.

Which brings us to yet another quality of Chibi's—in the words of our landlady, she was "a real looker." As the opinion of someone with a long history of chasing away stray cats, I figured she knew what she was talking about.

There's a photographer who says cat lovers always believe

their own cat is better looking than anyone else's. According to her, they've all got blinders on. She also says that, though she too is a major cat lover, having noticed this fact means that she is now hated by all other cat lovers, and so these days only takes pictures of scruffy-looking strays.

Chibi, who loved to play ball, gradually began to visit us on her own and would try and get us to play with her. She would step gingerly into the room and gaze intently at its occupants, then purposefully turn around and walk back out, as if to lead us to the garden. This process would be repeated until she got a response. Most of the time my wife would put down whatever she was doing, slip happily into her sandals and head outside.

Having played to her heart's content, Chibi would come inside and rest for a while. When she began to sleep on the sofa— like a talisman curled gently in the shape of a comma and dug up from a prehistoric archaeological site—a deep sense of happiness arrived, as if the house itself had dreamed this scene.

Avoiding the prying eyes of the landlady, we began leaving it up to Chibi to come inside the house whenever she wanted— and with this new development I had begun little by little to understand cat lovers. Whether on TV or in all of the ubiquitous cat calendars, it seemed as if there was no cat comparable to her. But, though I had started to think of her as the best cat around, she was not really our cat.

First we would hear the tinkling of the bell, and then she would appear, so we began to call her by the nickname "Tinker-bell." Whenever we wanted her to come over, this name seemed to find itself on our lips.

"I wonder where Tinkerbell is." By the time my wife had gotten the words out of her mouth we'd hear the tinkling of Chibi's bell. We'd realize that she was near at the point where, exiting the foyer next door (located at the second corner of Lightning Alley), Chibi would leap through the tear in the wire-mesh boundary of the property, dash along the side of the building, turn at the far end of the veranda, leap up onto the open area of the deck, and then, placing her front paws on the window frame at about the height of a human adult's knee, stretch out her neck to peek inside.

In winter she came inside. Little by little, through the crack in the partially opened window, her tendency to visit subtly developed; her appearances were repeated until, as if a silken opening in a fabric had been continuously moistened and stretched, Chibi had entered our lives. But at the same time — call it fate if you will — something else was closing in and pressing itself against that tendency.

4

IT IS NOT OUT OF PREFERENCE THAT I USE THE WORD fate—or should I say, *Fortuna*—but as the young cat's visits became more frequent, I came to feel that there were some things only this word could express.

The old mansion was built in the 1920s by a military man from Kyoto, and it is said that he brought in gardeners from the old city to work on the landscaping. The property was nearly five thousand square feet in its entirety, its long side stretching out from east to west. The garden was irrigated by a supply of water brought in on the south side and, with a variety of trees arranged about the grounds, boasted a design that made use of subtle changes in scenery as different flowers came into bloom with each season.

A pond, which received water cascading over a waterfall, was located in the center of the garden a little to the east, and there were two planters for water lilies—embracing more than one variety of the aquatic flower—embedded in the earth a short distance from the pond and near the veranda. In addition, there was a smaller cobalt-blue Chinese porcelain planter farther away from the veranda, at the edge of the pond, filled with the same black water and more water lilies.

I'd heard the landlady and her husband bought the house in the late 1950s. Their four children had, one at a time, each flown from the nest and since then the elderly couple had lived there, just the two of them, and the care of the trees and plants fell to the hands of the old man.

It was the summer of 1986 when we first visited the guesthouse, taken there by a realtor located right across from the train station. We had been forced to give up our previous rental quite suddenly, almost as if some kind of natural disaster had struck, and we were so completely exhausted that we had lost the will to search for a new home. So we'd asked an acquaintance to perform a divination, and we were told to follow the direction of fire (yang), the third calendar sign, which opens to fifteen degrees. Concentrating on this fairly narrow, fan-shaped area, with little effort, even unceremoniously, what we encountered was this place.

Passing through the shopping district with its old air and having gone up a slight incline, the area then descending toward the south was all residential. There was little traffic down the rambling slope though the road was wide: a large variety of plantings stood out against the background of the houses, and a calm atmosphere lingered there. The first time we entered this silence, a strange feeling of peace came upon me, as if a loving hand had placed itself gently upon my chest. It struck me that there seemed to be quite a large number of elderly people in the neighborhood.

Soon, to our left, the old house with the bamboo slats covering the bottom half of the plastered wall was pointed out to us, and then, ushered in under the gate, with its roof partially hidden by pine branches, my wife and I entered the little alleyway.

In his discussion of fate, it seems Machiavelli thought that *Fortuna* dominates at least half our lives, while in the remaining half or a little less, human strength and competence (*virtù*) attempts to counteract it. He imagined fate as a goddess, capricious and fickle, or as a river, which could flood at any moment.

Machiavelli—active in the politics of the Florentine Republic and known to succeeding generations for his political writings as the ultimate realist—was also a poet of rich and varied rhetorical flourishes. He left behind numerous poems, plays, and allegories. In his writings, extending across a wide range of literary forms, the theme of *Fortuna* and the word *virtù*—translated variously as competence, virtue, ability, skill, valor, grit, or backbone, and vigor, impulse, or momentum (only a sampling of the more than twenty possible renderings)—appear, and when in addition to these, the necessary, the essential, perhaps even desperate word *necessita* appears, a unique feeling of exaltation is communicated. *Virtù di necessita*—in other words, Machiavelli suggests that only the "skill displayed in times of emergency" can successfully compete with fate.

It is said that when comparing fate to a river, Machiavelli meant the Arno, which often brought floods to Florence. In his position as secretary of the government of Florence, he worked with Leonardo da Vinci, who had been hired as a military architect and attempted to realize a grandiose plan to change the natural course of the river. But the plan, initiated five hundred years ago, was plagued by misfortune—disasters both natural and man-made: it was a major failure.

In reading Machiavelli's literary works, of the many metaphors used to express fate, most especially meaningful is the river which could flood at any time—an image used in Chapter 24 of *The Prince*—perhaps because, having directly experienced such a major failure himself, he knew its sheer agony.

So let us liken fate to a destructive river here as well. The river rages, flooding the plain, consuming trees and buildings before it, washing away the earth and carrying it away to the other side. As it surges forward people flee, but ultimately they succumb to the water's momentum. Nothing—no one, escapes.

Living beings, in turning a corner, or in producing the movements required to enter the crack in a certain partially opened door, are endowed with certain properties, something which produces its own little river. These daily movements are repeated, and a certain tendency—a certain current if you will—is generated. Then this minor current, because it is a current, must at some point flow into a larger river. Not only in his political writings, but also in his poetry, plays and allegories, cannot Machiavelli perhaps be read as having, at bottom, this flow as the basis of his thinking?

5

THE KITCHEN-DINING AREA WAS SNUGGLED UP AGAINST the first sharp corner of Lightning Alley. From the window facing west above the sink, the big house's own kitchen window was visible, while on the opposite side of the cottage toward the east, our bay window in the dining room often revealed the heads of people turning the corner of the alley, visible just beyond the steel wire stretched across the top of the wooden fence.

Moving in a southerly direction through our guesthouse you first passed through the greeting area, a small space only two tatami mats in size, which looked toward the main entry on the right with its lattice door of frosted glass and, opposite that, the sliding door of a closet on its left. Once past this room, you arrived at a large Japanese-style room the size of six tatami mats. Entering, you first noticed the traditional tokonoma to the immediate right, while a closet took up the rest of that side of the wall. On the east side was a glass door, designed to look like a traditional latticework paper door through which you could see the backs of people beyond the fence who had just walked past the second lightning-shaped corner and were continuing on their walk down the alley.

Beyond the six-mat room was another room not quite as large, this one with a hardwood floor facing a little courtyard for drying clothes. The wooden fence continued beyond the miniature garden, turned, and came around, moss-covered, doing wonders to block the view from the landlady's impressive garden of goings-on at our place.

The cottage's design provided many windows. On the west side of the room with the hardwood floor, a round window with a vine-covered bamboo lattice was cut into the wall, leading one to believe it was originally a tearoom, or it may also have been a moon-viewing room as well. I'd been told that the view of the garden with its artificial hills had been best from here, but now it was obstructed by the addition of a bath, and the furniture of its residents had nearly destroyed the elegant design.

So many windows still had a relaxing effect on the weary. On the south side, running the full length of the room, there was a large window from knee-high up to the ceiling, which was nearly twelve feet wide and provided a sweeping view of the horizon. And yet, since the owner's garden wall ran on beyond the house, and as there were no real windows to speak of in the wall of the large neighboring residence to the east, and because of the natural features of the land itself with its downward southerly slope, no eyes fell on the interior. Partway out, the eaves—their outermost half of glass—hung over the garden and became an oblique skylight inviting in all the sunlight one wanted.

One day in early spring, 1987, six months after having moved into the new place, I opened wide the window with its aluminum sash and the wind came in from the south like an avalanche of snow. Then, one after the other, I opened all the other windows in the house. The window over the kitchen sink of course, and the glass lattice windows in the two bedrooms on the east side, followed by the bay window in the dining room and then the bathroom window. The house quickly became a hollow cavity for the wind to race through. I stared in blank amazement at the courtyard for drying clothes where the clouds in the sky ran quickly past. Two slender branches of mistletoe, which had been entwined there, snapped in the wind and fell. I looked up to see the neighbor's great zelkova tree, gradually encroaching on our side of the fence, blasted by the wind, causing both branches and trunk to sway violently. Through the slanted skylight, a few rays of sun would pierce for just a moment and then vanish, only to return, combined with buds blown in from the plum tree— everything timed to the rhythm of illumination and conceal-ment. The small desk had been toppled in the wind, scattering the various papers which had been placed there all about the room. Now, like beings with a will of their own, they rose up as if attempting to return to the place from where they had fallen.

Once the arrangement of objects had settled down, I felt that I was finally ready to establish myself in this place. "This is where I will live," I thought to myself. Perhaps it was because I'd now developed a feeling for the passing of the seasons in our new abode—as if each new house, each new neighborhood con-tained its own unique experience of the passage of time.

To the south side of the room with the hardwood floor, there was what they call in tearoom parlance a "hanging ceiling." This was where the slanting eaves of the roof outside ran into the interior, so that the ceiling on one side of the room shared the same slope. And this sloping ceiling of frosted glass, with slits like a bamboo screen, doubled the effect of the skylight. I would lie here on a woven mat, using my arm as a pillow, and await the changing of the light.

Spring rain began to fall. I found that I could observe the change in the size of the raindrops as if they'd been placed on a slide for viewing microscopic specimens if I closely watched the initial splatter of rain. I would also gaze blankly at the movement of clouds and the dancing of the great tree's leaves surrounding the house. The shadow of burnt rust passing by was the elongated belly of one of the thieving cats which would come and go from the property.

A bird would alight on the eaves and press its pink feet against the glass roof and just as soon begin to slide down its slippery surface. Taken by surprise, the bird would always quickly flee, making it to one of the wooden crosspieces in a few wingbeats. The translucent surface of the eaves caused unending confusion for the birds.

Time passed as I slowly built up the courage to resign from the publishing job I had kept for the last few years. Often work-related situations would find me out on the town where there was nonstop drinking, and then on the weekends I would while away the hours playing baseball—I began to feel that I was throwing away the time I needed to work on my own writing. The days seemed to rush by faster and faster, and my work as an editor, supporting the writing efforts of others, began to make less and less sense.

One day I found I had developed a large blister on my right upper arm, apparently caused by too much baseball. A few days later the blisters spread to my right shoulder, and then all the way up the right side of my neck. Then complications occurred. For a while my thought process became sluggish; speaking became difficult, perhaps because the nerves on the right side of the neck are related to the speech center in the left side of the brain.

As it turned out I had shingles. On one side of my body the virus had spread all along the nervous system. I underwent treatment for a month, but the nature of the disease is such that one never knows when one's condition might again be thrown out of order. And in the end, this is what finally encouraged me to make up my mind to quit my job. And yet all the same I was unable to build up enough courage to act on this plan. After all, there was no way I could make a living just on the projects I had accumulated up to that point. So I went from day to day in an atmosphere of gloom. But at the same time, something about having settled into our new place brought the expected challenges of the next year starkly before my eyes.

I approached my wife, who was in the kitchen—"Let's go to a café."

"Why do I have the feeling I don't really want to hear this?" She drew back, somehow knowing what it was I had to say.

At a little café in the old shopping district near the station, I laid a chart out on the table which I had drawn up showing the writing projects I had in process at the time, with per-page payments and royalties I could expect from each, and dates when payments could be expected. At the time my wife had a contract with a publishing company as a proofreader. Her job was to check the revised versions of galleys, first reading through the text without checking against the manuscript, then fact-checking and verifying references. She would also point out errors in translated texts, ensure proper usage of kanji characters, and in some cases improve on sentence construction. So I had her annual income added to the chart, and with all the data spread out before us, preached the virtues of having both of us work from home.

In any case, it looked as if we could handle our expenses for at least a year and a half. I myself knew that beyond that there was no guarantee, but in my role as seducer, I realized that absolute self-confidence was *de rigeur*, so I pushed ahead with my soliloquy, drawing a picture of our new life together—frugal, yet with the beauty of simplicity. She was still a bit nervous about the whole thing, but my wife, seeing the sheer effort I had made to get to this point, how painfully slow and careful my decision had been, couldn't bring herself to demolish the plan I had drawn up.

We went home and ate dinner, then returned to our desks placed side by side near the window on the south side of the house, taking up our own meager work. Before we knew it, it was the middle of the night. For no particular reason, my wife looked up and let out a muffled gasp of surprise. The full moon shone through the glass eaves above us with their slits like a bamboo screen, so that its image was drawn out, flowing there like a milky white river.

6

IT'S BEST TO GO EMPTY-HANDED. THIS WAS THE ADVICE of friends, all of them writers with whom I had worked over the years. Oddly enough, it was the fact of having supported first-rate work that eventually led me to give up my job. I'd always dealt with my writers with an honest respect, which came directly from me rather than from the demands of etiquette. They were almost like family in a way—distant yet close. All of a type, and several who came to me I looked after till their last breath. I myself had by this time passed my mid-thirties and was about to enter that territory called middle age, and here I was filling out the forms to officially leave my job.

I resigned from the publishing company in the summer of 1987. Now I was unattached, but in January of the following year, I received news that an old friend, with whom I had been close but hadn't seen in quite some time, was now apparently on the verge of death.

Though a bit older than me, Y. was a drinking buddy and one of my baseball friends. Most of all he was a poet of my generation and I had great respect for his many talents. He'd eventually married and two children were born. Next came a house in a northern suburb and when invited to play ball he'd come up with some kind of excuse, his voice trailing off almost painfully, so I stopped calling, and gradually we grew apart.

Over the course of time, always keeping a busy schedule as a production editor in the city and catching the last train home, he developed colon cancer, and in the spring of 1986, underwent hours of surgery. He was told—and friends were notified—that it was an "intestinal obstruction." Hailing from the snow country in the far north, he was hardworking and loyal. Soon after leaving the hospital he was back at work, returning to his usual habits, though on his commute he had begun using the handrail when taking the stairs at the station where he would change trains.

His poems were now rarely seen in the magazines. The noble-minded do not thrust others aside in order to make their way in the world. But then they themselves are ultimately thrust aside by the advancing tide.

When I rushed to the hospital to find Y. in his sickbed, he turned his face, swollen like a catcher's mitt due to the poisons in his system caused by kidney failure, and like a splendid beast maintaining its silent pride, managed a broken smile.

In the hallway the doctor informed me he had only two weeks left—"It's killing him," I thought. "And it'll kill you too. Never forget that ..." What was *it*? I felt I could see what *it* was quite clearly now.

But then something completely unexpected happened. The cancer cells, which had multiplied in the kidneys, underwent necrosis and were then discharged from his body along with urine. Miraculously, Y. recovered temporarily. And then, perhaps because of the strong painkillers, we were able to talk again like we used to when we were out drinking together—ostentatiously, with bravado—and he was able to joke with the visitors who came to see him. For someone like myself who no longer worked a nine-to-five job it was perfect. So for four months I visited dutifully, commuting to the suburban hospital as if I were dropping by one of the old watering holes we used to haunt.

During this time, Y. organized and arranged his complete works for a collected poems, which a group of friends had gotten together to produce. After the galleys were in hand, he even managed to write four new poems. Then, having dragged himself that far, he passed away in late May of 1988.

Looking back on it now, I'd say one's thirties are a cruel age. At this point, I think of them as a time I whiled away unaware of the tide that can suddenly pull you out, beyond the shallows, into the sea of hardship, and even death.

It was during that dark time when I learned of Y.'s dangerous condition that I discovered the strange optical phenomenon in our house. One day early in the afternoon I heard a voice calling from the kitchen. My wife, who had left her desk, was nowhere to be found. There was only a voice coming from somewhere around the first corner of Lightning Alley.

"Watch me from that little window in the kitchen!"

In the darkness behind the door of the toilet located in a corner of the kitchen, there was a space not quite three feet square, with a window hung like a projection screen, the only window in the house facing north, closed against the early spring chill. In the center of the polished glass, there was a perpendicular line of dimly floating green, which I became aware of now for the first time — perhaps a corner of the hardwood floor was reflected there. At just that moment the sound of footsteps slowly approached from the right, advancing purposefully, and my wife, in the form of an inverted image in vivid color, appeared from the left, stretched all out of proportion. As soon as the image appeared it disappeared to the right, passing in the opposite direction of the sound of footsteps.

Quickly I pulled open the window. There was a knothole in the wooden fence no larger than a coin. Placing my eye close to peek through, I could see the house on the other side of Lightning Alley and the high garden hedge. But the image in the hole was turned upside down.

I asked my wife to walk back and forth a few times outside the window, and we had some fun repeating our little experiment with this simple yet vivid illusion. Next I called my wife inside and I took her place in the street, walking back and forth so that she could see the visual effects. Then both of us sat on the raised platform of the two-mat-wide greeting area just inside the entry, eagerly awaiting the arrival of passersby, though this was a rare event on Lightning Alley. Like a camera obscura, which transmitted only that which was needed, the house with its breezy interior had a soothing effect on the soul.

7

I OFTEN REMEMBER THE APPEARANCE OF CHIBI THE CAT, and the scene in the guesthouse when she first came inside. It was in the late autumn of 1988. The Emperor's condition had deteriorated rapidly after he had vomited blood in mid-September and now everyone in Japan seemed to be in the mood for "voluntary restraint." There was a narrow space with an earthen floor for the washing machine facing the courtyard, which was a mere token of a garden partitioned off from the spacious garden of the big house. One shining, sunny afternoon, slipping through a crack in the open door, four bright white feet stepped softly onto the room's insulated drain board, and with a well-honed curiosity rushing through her entire body, Chibi quietly surveyed its meager interior.

The old landlady was constantly driving off the calico cat owned by the neighbors to the south. There was also a black bicolored cat, more a combination of India ink and a muddy color than burnt rust—an old alley cat who had managed to infiltrate the property. We heard that this cat would sneak into houses when people were gone if a sliding door was left open even a crack. My wife affectionately called her Mrs. Muddy.

Our lease stated clearly that no children or pets were allowed, but then one day the landlady told my wife that she was sorry she had worded it that way. Apparently, the elderly couple had simply wanted some peace and quiet. But their quiet life changed when the old man became older and weaker, and lay bedridden in the Western-style bedroom on the west side of the house, and then the landlady took on the burden of all the sundry chores of the entire estate until it was more than she could handle. Now she seemed to be attempting to take control of stray cats as well and rid the premises of them. Cats being cats, they could be found everywhere in the spacious garden, perched on a fence railing at some particular height, and she devoted herself to arbitrary searches and capricious measures ranging from the whimsical to the mad.

Once Chibi had learned how she could get into the little house, she would slip quietly inside as long as we left the door open a crack. She would never cause any mischief. She would simply stroll through the house in a leisurely fashion. Often she hid her soft body, with its pattern of lampblack spots floating on her pure white coat of fur, between the various objects in the room. She never made a sound. Nor would she allow us to hold her. If you tried to hold her she would let out a barely audible *mew*, bite your hand softly, and then slip out of your arms.

My wife was quick to reprimand such advances. Laughing at her husband with his bitten hand, she declared she would never hold Chibi—"She's a free spirit. She can do what she wants." So Chibi remained unfettered, coming and going as she pleased. Soon she began to sleep wherever she wished, in whatever position she liked.

From the end of that year—1988—till the beginning of the next, I struggled to complete the work of writing two books commissioned by a publisher. Other than one ring of the bell on New Year's Eve at the old Buddhist temple nearby and a brief pilgrimage to a Shinto shrine located in the opposite direction, followed by a visit to an all-night noodle shop, I took part in none of the usual year-end or New Year's festivities, but remained at my desk hard at work. The urgent work kept the atmosphere in the house tense till nearly dawn, but just when I had reached the point of exhaustion and was beginning to feel desperate, invariably, a small dim white shadow leapt onto the open veranda and, resting its front feet on the window frame, peered in through the large window on the east side of the room which the desks faced.

I opened the window and welcomed in the guest, accompanied by the winter sunrise, and the mood inside the house was restored. Chibi was our first New Year's visitor. They call the visitors who go around to all the houses on New Year's Day to wish everyone a happy new year "pilgrims." Curiously enough, though she didn't offer a prayer, when this pilgrim came in through the window she did seem to be familiar with at least one formal greeting—where the hands (or in this case the paws) are placed together on the floor to kneel before one's host.

So this is how the year began. And on the seventh of January, news raced through the Japanese archipelago that the Emperor had finally succumbed. Somehow by that time I had managed to write two books. Both of them were about baseball.

8

WE MADE A DOOR TO THE ROOM THAT ONLY CHIBI COULD get through, not any other cats. Below the large window on the south wall, there was a floor-level window of frosted glass about sixteen inches tall running the full length of the one above it, for sweeping out dust. By opening this window just three inches, a gap was left which allowed only Chibi to squeeze through. In order to prevent cold air and insects from getting in, we hung a thick cotton curtain of royal blue over it.

On the wooden floorboards in a corner of the Japanese-style room, we placed a cardboard box, which had originally contained mandarin oranges, to act as Chibi's own special room. We put a towel in the box and a dish for her food. Then we set a bowl for milk beside the box.

If Chibi happened to come in when the box had been moved to the other room for cleaning, she would immediately notice that it was missing, and then fall into a heap on the floor in confusion.

Her vermilion collar would occasionally be replaced by a lavender one. We never knew which collar she would appear in on any particular day. But Chibi seemed to know that she had an additional home where she would be cared for, even if by people not in a position to choose a new collar for her.

Once Chibi came over when two editors happened to be visiting. Aware of the strangers, she circled several times around my wife who was standing, as if to lay claim to her. She let it be known that we were now her caretakers.

One afternoon after the spring equinox had passed, Chibi had been out hunting. She arrived with a sparrow between her jaws. With her hackles up, she let out a howl and, aggressively stomping to make her footsteps heard, trotted around and around the guesthouse. I had heard that when a cat brings in a kill, it always brings it back to show its owners. It was almost as if the house itself was the subject of this display for Chibi, as she circled it many times over, yowling the whole time. Afterward she went to the vegetable garden on the far eastern end of the main garden and played with the unlucky sparrow until it no longer moved.

As she finished the poor sparrow's burial my wife repeated her earlier declaration—"I won't hold Chibi," she said. "It's more gratifying to let animals do whatever they like."

As April came round, gossamer-winged butterflies covered the garden, dancing just above its surface and coloring it a blue-gray. It seemed impossible for anyone walking in the garden to avoid stepping on them.

What's interesting about animals, my wife explained, is that even though a cat may be a cat, in the end, each individual has its own character.

"For me, Chibi is a friend with whom I share an understanding, and who just happens to have taken on the form of a cat."

Then she told me about a philosopher who said that observation is at its core an expression of love which doesn't get caught up in sentiment. By this time my wife's notebook had become a daily record of Chibi's activities.

In June I left my wife to look after the house and embarked on a tour: I had been assigned to write an article about several cities in the U.S. and Canada. It was during this time that a change apparently occurred in Chibi's behavior. Perhaps she had been well trained, but for whatever reason, Chibi never jumped up onto sofas or beds. She would even carefully walk around cushions meant for sitting Japanese-style on the floor of the tatami room. But then one night when my wife was asleep Chibi jumped up onto the covers and lay down beside her. Ever since, she was in the habit of sleeping next to her.

Meanwhile, I had caught a cold in the U.S., and as soon as I got home headed straight to bed. Chibi happened along, and as had become her custom, jumped up onto the covers, and only then noticed that a different person was there. She hesitated, and then jumped onto the mirror stand. After admiring herself for a moment in the mirror's reflection, she hopped down and disappeared into the darkness of the closet, slipping quickly by the strips of cloth hanging over the opening. The top shelf of the closet was her favorite place to sleep. Since it had no door we simply hung strips of cloth in front of it, so it was easy for her to come and go.

Chibi was able to sleep comfortably whenever she wanted. And from then on we got in the habit of laying out the futon early in the evening so that we too, the human residents, could sleep any time we wanted as well.

9

JUNE 21, 1989, IS THE DATE MY WIFE BROKE OFF HER friendship with Chibi.

My parents, who were visiting from Kyushu, brought my wife a gift—one of their local delicacies—giant mantis shrimp from the Ariake Sea, known as *shappa* in the local dialect. Removed from their package, their size was immediately evident—at least twice as big as what is served at the average sushi shop.

On their heads were two pairs of antennae—one large and one small—and they had five pairs of legs, the second pair of which, attached to the thorax, were especially large and shaped like a sickle or scythe, said to be used for capturing small shrimp and crabs. Their tails were shaped like large plates and used for digging holes in the mud along the shallows of the seashore. They were the color of topaz, and several iridescent violet streaks ran down their backs. If you poured boiling water over them, the purple streaks turned to bronze.

From the early summer catch, they also sported eggs, making them a highly prized delicacy. As soon as they were brought out for the evening meal, boiled and lightly seasoned, the sound of a bell could be heard, and the guest cat arrived.

Once she caught sight of the shrimp, Chibi could not contain her excitement. Her behavior was completely different from when she was offered fried fish or sashimi. But as always, my wife called to her and, tearing off a piece of shrimp with her fingers, extended her hand toward Chibi's mouth.

The fur on Chibi's back stood up like a shark's dorsal fin. Her tail swelled up like a raccoon's. Having finished off that morsel in the blink of an eye—perhaps it was the taste, or the texture, or how it went down so smoothly—she became all the more excited.

My wife offered her another piece. Again Chibi gobbled it up in an instant. At the table from the place opposite, you could see the red tongue in her mouth curl like a flame.

Chibi couldn't wait for the next mouthful. Perhaps the whole process had become too tedious, too painfully slow for her. I could see her slowly close in, inch by inch, her whole being focused on her prey. Her eyes narrowed like a warrior demon guarding the gate of an ancient temple, and on her front feet resting against the dining table you could see the claws become more visible.

"All right now, you wait your turn—" Almost before she could get the words out of her mouth, Chibi, having moved into a hunting posture, had sunk her fangs deeply into my wife's hand as she attempted to pull the shrimp away.

The blood began to flow. Then a voice more of anger than of pain burst forth—and now the spell was broken.

"Out! Get out! It's all over between us!"

The powerful impact of her voice frightened Chibi, who made a hasty retreat through the opening in the floor-level window. At first I thought it was funny that my wife addressed the little cat as if she were a close human friend, or even a lover with whom she was breaking things off, but later I realized she meant it.

"That bite was for real," she said, doing her best to endure the pain. At first I thought it was temporary, just a little spat over shrimp, but the wound was deep.

First she closed tight the floor-level window. Then she put away the royal blue curtain, the cardboard box, and the dish and towel, which had been inside it. On the next day, and the day after as well, my wife silently washed the paw prints off of the large window with an old piece of cloth.

Three days passed, and then in the middle of the night, a sound came from the large window, which had been shut tight. The sound was repeated over and over again. A soft, quiet sound. My wife walked over to the window from the tatami room and opened the curtain. Something was repeatedly bumping against the window with the same unchanging look in her eyes.

I took a peek at my wife's notebook around that time, and this is what she wrote — "It was small and white, with eyes wide open, like a bird striking a lighthouse."

10

A LITTLE AFTER NOON ON THE DAY OF THE TANABATA
Festival in 1989, there was a phone call from nearby—the ambu-
lette had arrived to pick up its passenger. With a quiet tension in
the air we went out to see them off.

The old man was placed on a stretcher and then put in the am-
bulette. It was a clear day, and he squinted from the glare of the
bright sun. The driver, wearing white gloves, folded the stretcher's legs and began a first attempt at loading it into the back of
the van designed for transporting the sick and elderly, but he had
the thing in backward and had to start all over again. The tired
old body, covered with summer bedding, was spun around once
in the road to perform the task. A group of high school students
in their navy blue school uniforms passed by, looking back over
their shoulders. The old lady, carrying only a small handbag, sto-
ically greeted each of the neighbors who had come to see her off.
Then the kerosene delivery man, who was normally seen only
coming and going as he sold his wares, drove up in his private car
to give her a lift. The old lady climbed into the front seat next to
the driver, an expression of restraint showing on her face as she
did her best to fight back her emotions.

When the two cars had disappeared over the hill, we stepped into the entrance of the main house for the first time. Now it was empty. We stood in the kitchen for a while chatting with the woman who had worked there as a housekeeper for many years, as if to soothe the melancholy of parting. After she left, we adjusted the lock on the new gate which had been installed for additional protection due to the lengthy amount of time the owners would be absent. Then we went back inside the house and inspected every corner of its interior, now almost bare of any kind of furniture, from closets to shutters. A small calendar had been left behind, attached to a pillar in the living room—the date July 7th remains inscribed in my memory.

From the veranda on the south side of the house we were able to look out over the spacious garden. From there it became evident that merely renting the guesthouse on the east side of the garden had given us no clue as to exactly how unique it was. Though the landlady had told us that we were free to stroll through the garden to which the old man had been so devoted anytime we liked, we had never gotten any farther than the eastern edge near our own house. Through the sliding glass door we could see the figure of the old man who had become immobile, lying completely still in his bed or at times seated in a rocking chair.

But the landlords were gone from the main house. The castle was without its lord.

Gazing out from the veranda of the deserted house, we could see that the wooden fence which acted as the boundary between it and the neighbors to the south had fallen into a state of advanced disrepair and, tilting, had been taken over by vines and creepers.

It took some time, but gradually the old woman realized it was impossible for her to maintain the garden on her own. The years of caring for her husband had taken their toll and, little by little, she had lost her drive. But even without that the question of death and inheritance had become imminent. She hated the idea of becoming a burden to others, not even her own children let alone strangers, so as she saw herself growing more feeble she had made the firm decision the year before to put everything in order at the house where they had lived for thirty years and to move to an apartment complex for the elderly which provided nursing care. Naturally this meant that she would have to eventually close up the rental as well. So if nothing else, it seemed fitting to make use of what time was left to us and enjoy the expansiveness of the garden.

When I went out to water the garden, taking hold of the hose and turning the spigot connected to the electric pump, a white-tailed skimmer dragonfly which was always seated on the same large rock beside the pond in a good place to catch the sun would float its pure blue body, brushed lightly with a layer of white, up in the air, and cautiously approach the stream of well water spurting from the mouth of the hose. I placed my finger over the opening to split the stream of water in two, making the arc suspended in the air larger and higher. Now there was enough distance so that the skimmer would not be frightened. It took flight then and approached the stream of water in midair, kissing it like a precision machine.

As this became my habit each morning, the skimmer gradually started to fly straight for the water as soon as I began spraying, and would stay there in the waterfall which hung in midair for a long while. I'd read in a book that the male of the species is solitary and tends to stake out a fairly extensive territory, and prefers being near water. Because of this I knew it must always be the same one. Just as I was about to utter the word "friend" he flew away. But I enjoyed his company while I could.

A wire laundry line was awkwardly stretched between nails on the guesthouse and on the big house for hanging out the wash. One day near the end of August, the blue skimmer was there on the line, still young and strong, copulating with a yellow female whose tail was raised and rested on his head, so that together they formed what looked like a bracelet in the shape of a distorted heart. When I approached them for a closer look they flew away without ever breaking formation and moved to a branch on one of the trees on the west side of the garden. Again I drew nearer in order to observe them more closely, and again the distorted heart danced away in the sky above my head.

11

I CONTINUED TO WORK IN THE GARDEN FOR RELAX-ation during writing breaks, cleaning reeds out of the pond, removing cobwebs from between rocks and trees, and pulling weeds, until the vast space with its folds and depth was trans-formed—now I was beset with the problem of how to main-tain it in that condition. Once I got into the details I ended up spending half of my day there. A professional gardener or land-scaper reaches a garden's overall harmony, but it did not look like I would reach that point very soon.

I couldn't help thinking about the fact that within a year the house and its garden would most likely be put up for sale. And yet despite that knowledge, I had begun acting as if I was a live-in groundskeeper, setting up house in a corner of the premises, large enough to be a public park.

I found I was frequently calling the old woman, now living in an apartment for the elderly out in the suburbs, to ask about every little thing. She would then ask me to look up numbers for her in the little phone book she had left behind, and sent me off on all kinds of little errands like picking up documents at the local government office and so on. Each time I would ask how

the old man was doing, but it seemed he was only getting pro-
gressively worse, and he was eventually placed in the hospital
attached to the eldercare facility.

Before she hung up the old woman would always remind me
that we were free to make use of the main house any time we
wanted. "And feel free to use the air conditioner," she would
say—until the familiar line changed to "use the heater"—it was
already late fall.

The old man died at the hospital. We heard the news from
their daughter, and then the old woman insisted that we attend
the funeral which was to be held near the eldercare facility. So
we ended up invited—landlord and tenant, the big house and
the guesthouse—a relationship which had gone on for barely
three years, and yet here we were, seated amongst the guests at a
funeral, as if we were distant relatives.

I pondered on how it was things had ended up this way.
There was of course a certain chemistry between my wife and
the old woman.... I don't know why, but for some reason they
got along extremely well. You could certainly say the old woman
was skilled at maintaining just the right distance despite living
on the same premises. But after all, it's not as if we were actually
family, so on the way home from the funeral we dropped by the
Tokorozawa ball park to take in a double-header, which, as it
turned out, was the decisive battle leading into the playoffs. Still
in formal black funeral attire, we did the wave as a couple for the
first time. But I somehow felt that even this was according to the
old lady's wishes. She would always point out to us the impor-
tance of being natural, of being ourselves. I remember one time

she dropped by for one of her occasional chats with my wife, seated on the top step of the side entrance. "So what if you don't have children. There's nothing wrong with that. You don't have to have kids if you don't want to. Just be yourself."

According to my wife, this could not have been mere consolation. There were echoes of some past misfortune, which led to this insight. And yet there were no signs that she had suffered excessively because of having had children. All four of them, whom we eventually met, both the two we'd chanced to meet at the house and the ones we were introduced to at the funeral, seemed to have grown into fine adults who had now established their own quite respectable households. Which made the old woman's words all the more mysterious.

Ever since that day, the day of the Tanabata Festival, I would leave the sliding glass doors on the veranda of the big house open in the afternoon to keep the place aired out. I brought the old man's bedside table from the Western-style room out onto the veranda to use as a desk, and sat deep down in the armchair that had originally been in the guest room, and began writing there on the veranda in a spot which gave me a clear view out over the garden. I avoided using the air conditioner even on especially hot days. I don't like air-conditioned rooms to begin with, and the structure of the house, with its extended eaves providing shade and the open Japanese-style rooms, did not require it.

In the empty air of the old manor, with none of the usual household objects to attract notice, one felt the presence of the house itself. Since it was not my own house, I felt enveloped in the thickness of its atmosphere—the sheer power of place.

Once I was called back to the guesthouse to take a phone call and left the main house empty for a while. When I returned, Chibi had come over from the neighbor's garden to play and was there inside the house. When she saw me, she quickly ran away. She never did that when she saw me at the guesthouse—it seems a whole different relationship sprung up between us when we met in a different place.

Settling into the old man's comfortable sofa for the long afternoon, I would watch the butterflies and bees buzz around the veranda. Eventually they would steal into the darkness of the parlor, then, drifting from room to room, would sometimes end up staying a long while. Once a Blue Admiral fluttered in, its implausible blue enhanced by its black wings, and sat for a while on the edge of one of the cushions. So that's how the year passed—1989, a year in which we entered a new era with its own new name—and summer dissolved into autumn and autumn deepened.

Even at night I continued to work amid the sounds of the insects. The view of the Kyoto-style garden, a collection of well-trimmed green hemispheres all piled up one on top of the other, was like a black-and-white photo in an old magazine of an author's all too perfect writing space, and hence unreal. But when I thought about how this place would soon be taken from me, I became extremely anxious and began to feel pressed to clear away all the work that had piled up.

Late one night, I heard the sound of someone at the front door, which should not have been opening. At the far end of the long hallway was the shadow of a man perhaps in his fifties.

While I was still unable to make out the figure in the shadows, whoever it was called my name, apparently to offer reassurance. "Oh, sorry, I meant to call first but ..."

It was one of the old woman's sons; we'd met at the funeral. He was one of the directors of a company in Tokyo, but lived down the coast a bit, a couple of hours outside the city. Our landlady had mentioned that he might occasionally stay over if it got to be late and he missed his train.

Out on the veranda, the old man's side table overflowed with mountains of books I had collected as reference material and piles of paper on which I had written notes and the beginnings of sentences and chapters. Aside from that, the entire house was completely empty, but the visitor was obviously at home as he removed his jacket and, somewhat inebriated, began loosening his tie. He seemed to be doing these things merely to make me feel less uncomfortable in my overly informal attire.

"Go ahead and keep working. Don't let me bother you." He seemed quite accommodating, but I put my things together and quickly retreated to the guesthouse.

12

CHIBI USUALLY BEHAVED COOLLY TOWARD HUMANS, and yet—when she came over from the neighbors to the east— she seemed completely transformed, sticking her nose into every corner of the expanse of greenery, intensely focused, plunging her front feet into things, jumping and prancing, and taking off running in circles at top speed as if she were completely out of control. After the old woman and the old man moved out, when none of the garden lanterns were lit and no lights were on in the house, this went on through the middle of the night till the wee hours of the morning.

The garden was like a forest to Chibi. Sometimes I'd go on long walks with her, watching her respond intensely to her entire surroundings, the energy rippling through her whole body: she would race recklessly around one particular area and then climb high up into one of the trees, exposing her body in midair as if about to veer off in another direction, trembling ... and there I was below, taking in the whole show.

So now we found ourselves in the unusual position of enjoying the full extent of the mansion and its grounds without paying a penny more in rent. I could play around to my heart's content with our little guest explorer, but as time would tell, this too would have to come to an end.

When the old man died in October, the old woman made yet another decision, and she assembled her four children to announce it. With the rapid rise in land prices in recent years, passing on the house to the children after she died would likely carry punishing inheritance taxes. So to avoid this, she felt it would be best to sell the property along with both houses while she was still alive. The deadline for the sale was set for August 1990. Considering the inevitability of my parting with Chibi, our nightly frolics became tinged with a certain sadness.

I concocted some schemes that would give us a way to stay there a while longer, but then realized that most of these were no longer feasible, given the rapid price inflation Japan had experienced in real estate over the past few years. It was this course of events that taught me the meaning of the word "subdivision."

In my mind I drew a line from north to south that would just barely allow the guesthouse to remain when the property was subdivided. If we could buy it, our life with Chibi would also be able to continue. But even a modest plot of that size would still be impossible for us to afford. Thoughts like this streamed through my head as Chibi stood at my side and just made it all the more painful.

One day, all of a sudden, the house she visits is closed up. She places her front paws against the window and peers in, but the interior is dark and empty. And the entrance is boarded up. In the days that follow she goes back to check a number of times. She presses her head against the window glass. But there is no one there. Soon a demolition crew comes to tear down this now obsolete and disused place ... but all this too is no more than the imaginings of a human.

I began looking for a new rental in the same area at a local realtor's office, but could find nothing appropriate in the vicinity. So, placing the zelkova tree at the center of the target area, and gradually widening my search in an outward-reaching spiral, I began searching for a new house in the vicinity that would allow us to keep Chibi.

I vowed I would work even harder to find the right place for Chibi. Overhearing me mutter to myself, my wife smiled a wry sort of smile—"Odd how you still refer to her as a 'guest' despite having become so attached."

13

NOVEMBER TOO HAD PASSED, AND THE FADED PURPLE OF
the garden's saffron was now waning—the same saffron which,
back when my wife was planting its bulbs, had caused Chibi to
creep up on her from behind and place one paw in a hole my wife
had dug as if to say "Let's dig some more!"

As autumn deepened, and the leaves of the zelkova were falling thickly, we moved into full-scale house-hunting mode. At
the same time, though we did not know why, Chibi's visits grew
more frequent. Moreover, the time she spent with us was longer—sometimes as much as half a day. Of course, aside from
eating in the cardboard box in the corner of the tatami room the
small mackerel my wife had fried for her and sitting on the desk
near the window gazing out at the scenery, her visits consisted
primarily of sleeping.

After watching her tiny figure leap past the mirror stand and
slip through the gap in the hanging strips of cloth onto the pile
of cushions on the upper shelf of the closet, I would leave her un-
disturbed for a while. Then, having judged the time to be right,
my wife would take hold of one end of the hanging strips of cloth
and peek gently inside. Often Chibi would be in the midst of

grooming herself, using her small, precise tongue, and would suddenly stop and look back over her shoulder at the intruder. Then after a while, when my wife had another peek, she would be nearly asleep, eyelids sagging and her body rolled up into a ball. Given a little more time, she would be sleeping peacefully, her white belly moving up and down with her breathing.

It was funny watching my wife looking between the strips of cloth to peep at Chibi. I could imagine Chibi's sleeping figure from her muffled laughter. It really was pretty funny—almost borderline weird.

Chibi came and went three times a day, staying for around three hours each visit. After the neighbors (her official owners) went to sleep, she would slip through the boundary hedge, and come over to this little house where the lights were still brightly lit. Then she would show that she wanted to play, and a game of ball would begin in the dark garden. After a while she would tire of the game and in the predawn hours retire to the closet and sleep. She seemed to find pleasantly comfortable the combination of this twilight nook with its human smell and the softness of the cushions.

The couple at work at their desks through the night would follow her lead and go to sleep, but then the small guest would again awaken by 7:40 A.M. at the latest and eat the food which had been prepared for her in the cardboard box and drink up the milk in the saucer placed beside it, and quickly leave.

Later we learned that the reason for her morning rush was that she would always see off the little boy when he left for nursery school. Wandering in the abyss of half-sleep I would sometimes

hear the spirited voice of the boy and his mother's repeated re-
minders to be careful, which he obviously ignored, as the two
parted at the corner of Lightning Alley. Despite the early hour,
Chibi would always be there, standing and waiting at the corner,
and then run after the boy a little ways to see him off each morning. Mixed in with the voices of mother and child would be the
sound of Chibi's bell, and this is how I knew that she was there.

After she was finished seeing off the boy, she would continue
her carefree inspection of the garden, fanning out into a broader
range of ground. At various points she would go back to her own
place at the neighbors and eat. Perhaps she had more catnaps
planned for this time of day as well. Occasionally before we even
got out of bed, she would already be back over at our place asleep
on the cushions in the closet, having pulled open the strips of
cloth with her paw and jumped back in.

After getting up late in the morning, my wife would pull open
the strips of cloth and peek in at Chibi. "Don't you think she really belongs to us?" She seemed especially pleased about that
prospect as she gazed at Chibi's sleeping figure.

Eating and sleeping as much as she liked, circulating freely
between locales, it seemed as if the boundary between the two
households had itself come into question. Even the words we
used to talk about Chibi had become a mass of confusion: was
her coming to our house a return—a homecoming—or was it
the other way around? Was home really over there? The whole
situation seemed to be in flux. Once, when we had been out for
the day, we returned to find Chibi there in the dim light of the
entrance to welcome us, seated properly, feet together on the

raised wooden floor as if she were a young girl who had been left to care for the house while we were away.

"See, I told you. She's our girl."

… or so my wife said, though she knew she wasn't really ours. Which is why it seemed all the more as if she were a gift from afar—an honored guest bestowing her presence upon us.

14

EVEN AFTER HER VISITS BECAME MORE FREQUENT CHIBI never let out as much as a *meow*, and she would not let us pick her up.

It was summer. Late in the night, after we had fallen asleep, came the sound of the scampering of feet—unusual for Chibi to be running around like that at that time of the night. She had jumped up onto the nightstand covered with a tablecloth, which had been pushed over near the window when we laid out the futons before bed. From there she suddenly jumped onto the screen over the open window and was hanging there by her claws. I realized now that something was wrong.

She remained fixed high up on the inside of the screen like a tropical lizard, extending her neck, trying to look over the fence between our yard and her own house. Even in this fix she made no sound. Finally my wife thought of something: she went into the other room to check the floor-level window and discovered that it was closed. On the previous night, Chibi had entered through the front door, which was unusual, and we had inadvertently left her private entrance closed. I often remember now how my wife, an eccentric in her own right, ever since then referred to the cat door as "Chibi's nostalgic passageway." (Her longing for a way home?) I suppose the screen incident was a roundabout way the world had of telling my wife that Chibi was, after all, not ours.

That fall we took delivery of a package for the neighbors while they were away. Once she had determined that they were back, my wife took the package over to them. The front door was left open, so she rang the bell and stood in the entry waiting for someone to appear, but it was Chibi who came to greet her rather than the lady of the house. My wife was stunned. Chibi, who had been coming over to our house every morning and every night for who knows how long and had never let out a sound, now, for the first time, opened her mouth and began expressing herself at great length. The content of her speech—or so my wife reported to me with the utmost seriousness—was not about thanking us for taking care of her all of the time but rather, the usual social niceties, chatter about the weather and so on, and all the other insincere politenesses that neighbors often exchange.

Even for my wife, who to all appearances seemed to have such a rapport with Chibi, this was the only time she made her voice heard. And of course her reserve went without saying when it came to adult males, from whom Chibi always kept a certain distance.

When winter came, I was over at the big house one afternoon in the underground storage space attached to the kitchen to stow away some large containers of kerosene. I pulled open the wood panel, which acted as a door, and went down and suddenly there was Chibi, who had come down behind me. She walked leisurely across the concrete, which had been added to provide a firm footing in the space, and then jumped up onto one of the shelves. With her front feet neatly aligned on her perch, she began to observe the procedures as they unfolded. As I waited for the automatic pump to finish transferring kerosene into the small space heater (there was of course no central heating in the old house), I tried imitating the way my wife would often talk to Chibi, making her words into a little song—"*Together just we two, down below the ground . . .*"

In response, Chibi crouched down, feet still placed together, and shaped her mouth as if about to roar like a savage beast, all the while glaring at me fixedly. Meanwhile, she gathered herself as if she were about to pounce. Perhaps it was a form of intimidation meant as a proper young lady's preemptive strike against a potential molester.

On another day, she came bolting through the open door facing the little garden of the guesthouse like a bullet, and immediately hid in the tiny space between some furniture and a small storage box. With her backside facing me, she was shaking so hard I felt sorry for her. When I turned toward the door there was Cal, the calico cat that belonged to the neighbors to the south, eyes blazing, ready to pounce. Somehow this attack on Chibi looked to be more jealousy-based than territorial, perhaps because Chibi came and went as she liked between the two houses. I had noticed that there was some dispute going on between them a few days earlier when I had rescued Chibi from a branch high up in a tree where he had her cornered.

Cal was an impressive calico. But only Chibi was allowed inside, which may have been what led to the recurring cycle of attacks. The more she was attacked, the more cautious and fearful she became, while Cal's behavior became increasingly bold. "He's probably absolutely cute and lovable when he's at home next door," said my wife. So she began calling his name and talking to him a bit when he appeared in the garden so he wouldn't feel so jealous.

Mrs. Muddy seemed to be in same class as the old lady (for she was getting on in years now). Her fur had a pattern of India ink and mud-colored splotches, but her eyes were large and translucent, and she had a calm disposition, even a cozy air of nostalgia about her. I suppose she had reasons of her own, something in her past perhaps, that made her find ways to open the doors and windows of people's houses. Old alley cat that she was, she must have been in the situation at some point in her life where she'd had a home.

One night when my wife was home alone, she sensed the movement of the cloth hanging over the floor-level window and heard the sound of cat feet, which always meant that Chibi had arrived. But when she turned around, there was Mrs. Muddy. The window must have been left open wider than usual. When their eyes met, both Mrs. Muddy and my wife were surprised, and the old alley cat turned right around and ran out, bumping into the side of the cat door on the way and making a loud noise.

My wife provided a vivid description of the event. "It was pretty funny," she said, "but I felt a bit sorry for her." Strangely enough, Chibi and Mrs. Muddy seemed to get along.

Once my wife saw the two of them out in Lightning Alley, Mrs. Muddy rolling around on the ground showing her big white belly and Chibi directly above her perched on the wooden fence. Mrs. Muddy then ran into the bushes lining the neighbor's property to the north, and Chibi followed in close pursuit. The two disappeared into the darkness and it was quiet.

After a while Chibi came over to the house alone, and my wife put the question to her—"Are you friends with Mrs. Muddy?"

Perhaps it was because she was the age of one of the old woman's granddaughters, but in any case, my wife and the landlady seemed to have no disagreements in particular. My wife says that on another day she saw Chibi and Mrs. Muddy together for a long time, deep in conversation on the other side of the wooden fence on the north end of the property, just below the knothole through which the images of passersby always appeared.

"They weren't meowing together, in a matter-of-fact way. It seemed more like they were intimately discussing their personal lives." She tilted her head to the side as she spoke, as if not quite believing her own words.

A few days passed after Chibi had raced like a bullet into the house running from Cal. It was late morning on a January day and my wife was alone in the house. After she awoke she began to prepare breakfast when Chibi emerged from the closet and jumped down onto the tatami mat floor. She stood still there for a while—something wasn't right. Some of the white fur on her back was torn out, and through it you could see the red-colored skin. Chibi looked up at my wife for a while and then slowly returned to her place next door.

It appeared that she wasn't injured badly, so my wife calmed herself and returned to her desk where she had a rush job waiting.

In less than fifteen minutes Chibi was back. She had gauze bandages wrapped around her torso. She jumped up on the desk as if to say, "look what happened to me." Then she sat down, exposing her helpless figure to my wife, and gazed at her with a feeble expression.

My wife gazed back. Then she thought of how they would soon have to part, and all the conflicted feelings came rushing in. "After all, she isn't really ours. . . . But maybe I wish she really were. . . ." Chibi stared intently with her deep green eyes at the clear liquid flowing from my wife's eyes and rolling down her cheeks—these human things called tears.

15

THE YEAR 1990 ARRIVED AND ALREADY IT WAS THE MID-
dle of February. She always appeared during the day, but why
was it she came again at night? It must be because the family she
lived with next door went to bed early. It had become one of my
wife's greatest pleasures in life to go out into the garden to greet
Chibi no matter how busy she might be at the moment and no
matter how cold the weather.

Chibi would climb her favorite tree, a smallish pine in the center of the garden. If you tossed a Ping-Pong ball to her, she would
jump quickly into action like a volleyball player on the attack,
and complete a perfect spike. Chibi never tired of this game no
matter how many times it was repeated.

At night my wife would follow Chibi wherever she wanted
to go on the grounds of the stately mansion. Sometimes they
would end up mounting the stairs into the main house itself.
With almost no furniture left, the house was like a great hollow
shell of darkness.

Next to the raised alcove in the parlor was a study in the grand
old style. Moonlight passing through the paper screens bathed
the room in a soft lunar glow. With her back to the source of

light, she tossed the Ping-Pong ball to Chibi, who waited at her leisure on the built-in desk. Chibi batted it back and the game continued for so long my wife lost track.

Soon the shapes of things became more visible in the moonlight, bolstered by the lights shining in the guesthouse and the light in the entry of the main house which was always left on to guard against burglars. In the twilight of the big house, the white ball reflecting the moonlight could be seen dancing in the air, and its sound hitting the hard surface echoed through the halls. As she danced along with the small sphere Chibi was clothed in moonlight.

Chibi now played all day in the garden, which showed the first stirrings of spring's energy and chaos, rolling in the plum blossoms, getting the petals stuck in her fur, swatting flies, sniffing lizards.

Suddenly climbing a tree she would transform herself into lightning. Normally lightning travels down from the sky, but Chibi ran up. My wife wrote in her notebook of the electrifying speed with which Chibi climbed the persimmon tree—"like the tip of a lightning bolt," and elsewhere, "as if arousing the thunder." And indeed, that's exactly what it was like.

She brought to mind a passage from the *Nihon Shoki* (Chronicles of Japan), which describes the god of hunting. The classical text reads: *Before the gate, at the foot of the tree that stands near the well, there is a rare guest. By his countenance I think he is not common. If he is descended from heaven he should have a heavenly face, and if he is of the earth his face too should be earthly. Truly this is a great beauty. Might he be a prince—an heir to the imperial throne?*

Her figure, balanced on a branch at the top of the persimmon tree she had dashed up, carefully gauging the wind, bracing herself for its next movements, seemed to have separated itself from both heaven and earth, projected into a space that was ultimately dimensionless.

I'd heard that cats offer their complete trust only to the people who are feeding them. So they only reveal their really cute side to their owners. Hence it follows that we—the odd couple living next door who were not really Chibi's owners but were merely getting a taste of what cat ownership might be like on an ad hoc basis—were most likely not shown her most coquettish behavior.

But that also meant that Chibi was willing to show us another side of her personality which she didn't show her real owners—her true nature, her refusal to pander to humans, the untouched, wild part of her character. This is where that sense of mystery that Chibi always left us with came from. I think a prime example was that part of her that I name, for lack of a better term, "Lightning Catcher."

This was the title of a legendary series of works in color lithograph and encaustic by a painter who had started his career in copperplate engraving. I was invited to a retrospective focusing on his prints held at a small privately run museum in a part of Tokyo consisting mostly of abandoned industrial warehouses. I also gave a talk with the artist.

What did "Lightning Catcher" mean to the artist? The series of works arose out of many years of the artist's exploration of color—the idea seemed to literally jump right out at him from the classic splashed-ink paintings of the Kanō school. In these works, color comes into existence out of the materials and the very atmosphere itself, followed by the image, ever-changing, vital, raw ... the work attempts to capture the actual instant, that site of the excruciating birth of the image.

The conventional assumption is that a painter extracts colors and images from nature, fixing these elements on a surface to produce a completed work. But in this case, the painter refuses to fix the images, these being no more than the constant change and movement of matter and air. In other words, the artist steps directly into nature and attempts to capture the actual flow of color and image. In a certain way this makes him akin to Leonardo da Vinci.

Toward the end of our talk I mentioned the fact that the characters making up the title of the series could be read in either of two ways—"a process which catches lightning" or "the capture of something quickly (with lightning speed)." The artist simply laughed and would not specify which reading was the correct one. The third member of the discussion was an art critic, and our opinions differed on this subject. What I suggested was that, according to my sense of the language, the simplest and most literal interpretation is the first, while the second, less standard reading implies the act of capturing something with movements like lightning.

There were two series of prints under the same title. One made use of encaustic, in which color pigments are added to hot beeswax and then applied to prepared wood rather than canvas. The artist must apply the quick-drying, syrupy substance and instantaneously capture the image. This Lightning Capture process was performed in monochrome.

The next series made use of color lithography. Colors are applied over a slate palette and fluctuate, shifting dimension as they appear. What the artist attempts to capture in this approach is the fluctuation itself, the shifting between dimensions.

At the risk of belaboring a point, the first method in which the artist attempts to capture something with lightning quickness would be "lightning capture," while the second, in which the attempt is to capture colors which appear like lightning, would be "capture of lightning."

Going by this definition, Chibi's lightning moves in the deserted garden would be of both kinds. In other words, this cat was as quick as lightning, and at the same time was doing her best to catch the lightning.

Later, as I gazed at the collection of paintings reproduced in the museum catalogue, I noticed that beside the title there was an English translation, most likely provided by the artist himself. I was completely taken aback—the translation read "Catcher of Lightning." In other words, rather than the object, it was the subject of the action that was being pointed to. But if this were the case, wouldn't the reading change yet again? Perhaps this time with a different accent, and, like Chibi, ears finely pointed, twitching to stirrings off in some unknown direction, as the tongue alights softly on each syllable ... or at least that's how I imagined it.

The wooden storage shed which stood on the southeastern end of the garden had a rough frame, its primitive door made of wood and wire mesh. The old man, who had loved working in the garden, kept the tools here for gardening and woodworking, including a stepladder and a net for cleaning the pond. He had studied metallurgy at the old Imperial University before the war, and had left surveying equipment and drafting instruments used in mineral exploration and geological surveys tucked away in the nooks and crannies of an old desk which had been demoted from the big house and left in there.

Below the roof of the shed were the crossbeams that supported it, and some planking which spanned the beams, creating a raised platform. This was another one of Chibi's favorite spots. Resting from her *lightning capture* activities, she would gaze outside from her perch on the end of the planking, paws tucked comfortably under her chest. In this position, she faced the guesthouse, looking squarely in the direction of my desk.

One afternoon as I worked at my desk facing the window, I heard my wife's voice coming from the garden. It was an almost mournful sound. I could only see Chibi since my wife was hidden behind the wooden fence, but apparently she was looking up at Chibi where she sat between the shed's roof and the crossbeams. It seems she was telling Chibi that we would soon have to part with her.

"Do you understand? Do you have any idea what I'm talking about?"

Chibi acted as she always did. Her interest was in her own natural talents, and the animal and plant kingdoms. The human world was of no concern. She simply cocked her pointy little ears in the direction, hidden to me, from where those sounds were coming, as they indiscriminately spread throughout that corner of the garden and then dispersed.

16

MARCH ARRIVED.

On a Saturday evening, the two of us hurried under a nearly full moon to the opening reception being held at the gallery for the painter of "Lightning Catcher," heading down Lightning Alley in the direction that cut east. The gallery was not really that far, but the train would take us on a roundabout route back into the city center, a trip which would require an hour to complete. The shortest and most direct route would be by bicycle, which would have us arriving in only thirty minutes.

Holding our bicycles we passed through the small side gate and pushed them as far as the lightning-shaped corner where we turned. There at the boundary of the next door neighbor's house, we saw Chibi slip through a tear in the wire mesh covering a gap in the wooden fence. As soon as she touched ground she turned her back toward us and circled around toward the southern, outer wall of the guesthouse, traveling through the slender fibers of the wild grass. From there we imagined her alighting on the open veranda, then passing through her private entrance in the floor-level window, which only she could get through, and finally entering the room with the wooden floor.

We had never before seen her on her border crossing from that angle. And we had never seen her heading toward our house from behind. My wife and I looked at each other as if to say *so this is how she slips quietly out of her own house and comes over to give us a visit.* The desire to go back home flitted across the back of my mind, but was crushed in the end by the need to go.

At the gallery, an opening party was being held where one could meet and talk with the artist. Since I had written something for the catalogue, I had been sent a small original print by the artist as a gift. But somehow I felt ill at ease.

After the opening party we had coffee with close friends—a book designer and an editor. I told them about our situation, how we would soon be forced to move, and told them about the cat who visited us repeatedly. I guess I just let open the floodgates, even telling them about how my last ray of hope was that I might win the lottery so that we could buy the guesthouse. I explained that in reality, the land likely cost three times more than what we could ever afford, even on the off-chance that the owners would be willing to divide the property so that our little house would be left on its own.

At 9:30 we left the coffee shop and again mounted our bikes, one following the other like a miniature caravan, and thirty minutes later arrived at Lightning Alley, entering from the back way on the east side, and finally returned home.

Evidence of Chibi's having come over while we were out was scanty, but there were definite traces. For instance the cat food placed in the dish inside the cardboard box had decreased somewhat in volume. "I didn't put in any of those little fried mackerel this time," said my wife, as if in explanation for her having eaten so little, and began frying some up. But that night Chibi didn't come for her usual midnight snack. Nor did she come Sunday.

"She's gone to see her aunt at the beach house," said my wife: "She's gotten in her basket and taken a little outing."

She seemed satisfied with her own explanation. After all, Chibi had been away for a number of days during the summer last year for much the same reason.

"And she'll wear a little straw hat, you know, like the elementary school kids, because it's the weekend, right?"

On Monday it rained heavily and a strong wind blew. Around noon a patch of blue appeared briefly between the dark clouds, and then after a while the weather improved. The chattering of the Japanese bush warblers resounded throughout a broad patch of ground in the center of the garden. The sound of drums came from the neighbor's house. The sound was especially loud and intense, and lasted for quite some time. "So it's not the whole family that's away," I thought to myself. Chibi didn't come on this day either.

"So Tinkerbell's not coming, eh?"

The words I had been trying to avoid saying slipped out of my wife's mouth, and gradually they began to recur with more frequency. My wife, who had difficulty hearing Chibi's bell, asked me repeatedly if I had detected any signs of its approach.

Time passed and the mackerel were thrown out. Then my wife prepared a new batch.

Right at the point where it had become unbearable a friend called up from a bar in Shinjuku, one of the major entertainment districts in the city, its narrow labyrinthine alleys lined with numerous little drinking spots, and suggested I come out to meet him, "and bring the wife along." The invitation came at just the right moment. We stayed out drinking until the early morning hours. It seemed the longer we stayed out the better our chances were that she would appear. Meanwhile, we could escape the painful hours of waiting for her when she simply wouldn't come. But it seemed more as if we were just getting our insides all twisted up.

Together we pulled an all-nighter, arriving back home the next morning. There were no signs of her having visited, a fact which was ascertained when we were awoken after only three hours of sleep by the mailman carrying an express package.

We could hear each other breathing. By nightfall the interior of the house felt like an invisible body of water about to overflow its banks and inundate the surrounding area.

So that my wife would not detect me, I went over to the main house and allowed myself to use the ancient phone—the old analogue kind with the dial they had when I was a kid, for some reason always the color black, and surprisingly heavy. I dialed the number of the neighbor's house, which I had just looked up, and the boy answered with his usual gusto, saying *nobody's home*.

"And the cat?" I managed to blurt out.

"It died," he said, with no change of tone.

"When?" I asked.

In the same energetic voice he answered, "Sunday." When I pried further for an explanation as to why, he said he didn't know.

Or perhaps he just didn't understand, because of his age ... I don't know ... the meaning of death. Anyway, that's all I got out of him, all delivered in the same monotonously cheerful voice.

One by one I furiously closed the shutters of the main house, and putting on the wooden clogs I had worn on the way over, noisily returned to the guesthouse over the hard-packed clay surface of the walk. In a voice that was partly a shout, partly a sob, I announced the horrible news to my wife.

17

THERE WERE SIGNS THE LADY OF THE HOUSE NEXT DOOR
had returned from her shopping expedition. I left my wife at
home broken down in tears and in moments found myself turning the corner of Lightning Alley and then ringing the bell at the
entry of the neighbor's house. Until that moment my dealings
with neighbors had been limited to passing each other in the alley or exchanging polite greetings when taking over a package we
had kept for them while they were out. I had never made a real
visit or actually had a conversation with them before.

"It seems she was hit by a car last Sunday night. But there were
no external wounds. She just lay there in the street with such a
calm expression on her pretty face. That's what was so strange."

Her use of the word "strange" seemed right on the button to
me. Chibi was indeed a strange cat ... uncanny really. I found
myself getting a bit giddy sharing this with someone, despite the
fact that it was Chibi's owner.

"You know, when we first found Chibi she wasn't here in the
alley. Chibi first appeared to us out on the main street, just up
the hill a ways, toward the station. It was in front of the house
with the Japanese plume grass growing near the entryway. After

we found her she ended up following us all the way home. Then when I went out to look for her last Sunday that's where she was, lying dead in exactly the same place where we first found her. I never go that way on my own except when I go shopping and have my boy along with me. Late at night—I think it was around eleven-thirty—someone came by and asked me about it, saying "Isn't that your cat?" ... so I rushed out ... and that's where she was, in exactly the same spot where we first found her."

Practicing what seemed like an immense amount of self-control, she continued in her soft-spoken manner.

"It was so late at night, and since it was a holiday the clinic wasn't open ... and my eldest son was on the respirator till morning so I couldn't depend on him to help out ..."

I was aware that they had a high-school-aged son also. He must have been the one who was playing drums the other day.

"I buried her at the foot of a little pine tree in the garden."

So they have a pine tree in their garden too, I thought to myself. I had never gotten a look at their garden since Lightning Alley's sharp twists and turns meant that the property was too far south to be directly in our view. There was a small apartment building, apparently some sort of corporate housing, which could be approached only via a private road by circumventing the alley and passing through an iron gate. It would take some courage, not to mention skill at coming up with excuses, to pass through the gate, climb the apartment stairs and get a look at the garden from that angle.

Then her voice became even softer as she spoke again in a wistful tone: "She had a good life. I think she was happy."

"Chibi often came over to our house to play. My wife really doted on her."

"Oh, is that so … well, thank you."

"She would fall asleep at our place, but she would always wake up at the same time each morning. Apparently that was when your boy left for school. She would always go out to see him off."

"Oh, really … thank you so much."

She bowed politely to me. The way we were talking it sounded more like a human child had died. I wanted to talk some more. I really felt like suggesting we talk some more when we both had some time and share all those things about Chibi the other didn't know—about the two sides of her personality. Words to that effect found their way as far as my throat but then stuck there. Countless scenes of Chibi sprang up in my head which had become special memories, but just as the words began flowing out I found myself holding back.

"Would you mind if we visited her grave sometime … I mean, when it's a good time for you of course."

"Oh, why certainly, yes. Can you give me a call tomorrow morning? It's already getting a bit late."

I wonder where it all comes from—this need to go to the place where the body has been laid to rest. It's the need to reconfirm how precious someone was and how irreplaceable, and the desire to reconnect with them on a different plane.

18

ON WEDNESDAY MORNING I BARELY MANAGED TO GET two hours of sleep. I think my wife slept even less. When I got up I found her out sitting on the veranda looking at nothing in particular. I spoke to her and then went out into the sunny garden to cut a few branches of plum, *Daphne odora*, and daffodils. The garden just didn't seem the same. It wasn't our garden anymore. It had lost all its energy and spirit. Seeking signs of Chibi which might have remained, I took pictures here and there in the garden.

I waited till after nine o'clock, and as promised, put in a call to the neighbor's house, but nobody picked up. I tried a few more times but still no answer. I called again after eleven and the missus answered the phone.

"Sorry to disturb you at a time like this ..."

"Oh, no ... not at all ..."

"Would it be possible for us to just briefly leave some flowers?"

"Oh, I'm sorry, but can I get back to you some other time?"

The woman's nearly inaudible voice gradually emerged between sighs. Her tone had completely changed since yesterday when she'd told me in a silken voice that she would see how things go. Her voice didn't exactly trail off. It was quiet, yet commanding. It had the tone of someone who, having thought it all over without sleeping the night through, had given her final answer and would not budge.

The flowers I had cut hung suspended in midair.

"So it looks like we can't visit the grave."

My wife cried some more. We both became desperate. As long as things remained as they were, we would be unable to take possession of the imaginary path we needed to reconnect with Chibi. I tried getting a look over the fence behind the toolshed in the southeastern corner of the property, but I couldn't get a good view of the neighbor's garden at all, let alone the pine tree where Chibi was buried. We left the plum, *Daphne odora*, and daffodils in Chibi's little cardboard box in the corner of the tatami room.

We need to explain to her that we didn't forcibly bring Chibi in, I thought. She came in on her own, and we played with her without really thinking anything about it. And then Chibi began taking little naps here. We always let Chibi do as she pleased . . . we didn't even touch her. We have to explain that to her.

Little by little I began writing about our history with Chibi in the form of short essays, and publishing them in a quarterly magazine with a limited distribution. I placed two or three issues of the magazine in an envelope along with a letter and mailed it.

My wife couldn't keep any food down. She just couldn't get over the fact that Chibi was already dead when she'd cooked up more fish to put in her bowl. As I watched my wife languishing away, I began to feel it would be best not to move too far away. On the other hand, we were no longer in need of a place close enough for the cat to come visit. But if we could just find a place with a view of the zelkova tree … and since this was a neighborhood where high-rise buildings were not allowed, a tree of that size should be visible from quite a distance, certainly from a second-story window, and definitely from anything higher than that.

Below the zelkova tree time had stopped. At the foot of a little pine tree in its shadow, the most important of gems lay sleeping. Perhaps a window with a distant view of that place would allow us to yield to the natural process of forgetting.

I went to the library and opened a book on geometry for the layman. I looked for the section on triangular surveying. There was a diagram providing a simple explanation of a method of surveying devised by people in ancient times. This was the simplest way possible. To find an object's height, measure its shadow at the very moment when the length of the surveyor's own shadow equals his actual height.

According to another method, a stick is set upright near the object whose height is to be measured. Between the two objects are two imaginary triangles equal to each other. The ratio of the height of the object to be measured to the height of the stick is identical to the ratio between the lengths of the two shadows. From this fact one can calculate the height of the object.

Either of the two methods could easily be performed in the garden during the morning hours when the sun shone in from the east. These are thought to be the methods used by Thales of Miletus to measure the height of the pyramids. There was only one difficulty in performing the task—the requirement that the length of the pyramid's shadow be measured from the center of its lowest point.

This corresponds precisely to the difficulty I faced in measuring the zelkova tree. Mainly, it would be impossible for me to measure the zelkova's shadow from its exact center position, since of course I could not get into the neighbor's yard. However, the problem could be solved by making use of a map drawn to scale, produced with the use of high-precision surveying.

Knowing the measure of the top of the zelkova tree, one could then go on to figure the location of the apartment and window required to obtain a view of the tree. In addition, one would of course have to obtain the heights of local topography and therefore the heights of windows, and then draw an imaginary triangle. Since windows and the gentle rise of some of the neighborhood streets do not produce shadows, one would be required to use the following method: the surveyor looks up and points to the thing he would like to measure, then he measures the angle from that point to the position of his arm when pointed horizontally, and with this angle, the coordinates of the peak of the triangle, the length of each of its sides, and the azimuth angle can then be determined. Finally, one adds the height of one's eyes.

Next one draws a straight line that connects the top of the zelkova tree with the window of the new apartment. From this one can calculate the height of any obstructions to one's view. If an obstruction is located directly in the line of sight, this means that—whether it be a building, a patch of greenery, or the shape of the land itself—the zelkova tree will not be visible from the window in question. Therefore, in the strategic zone between viewing point and target the high and low points of the terrain must first be determined. The search area will of course be limited to that zone in which the zelkova tree remains visible.

But perhaps I had embarked on this line of thought merely to distract myself from my own anger and grief. It's not as if I was actually prepared to waste my time attempting to perform triangular surveying. I was merely seeking comfort in the thought that something as serenely transparent as an ancient surveying method might be applicable to this place of loss and bewilderment where I now found myself.

19

IT WAS AROUND THIS TIME THAT I BEGAN TO REALIZE how thoughtless I had been in sending over what I had written about Chibi.

That series of essays, though shorter and in a recognizably different style, was essentially a rough draft of what would later become the first part of this novel—the first three chapters in which the cat appears and begins to stay a while and play. I was beginning to get the feeling that by having sent the neighbors those magazines I had merely raised suspicions.

But this isn't all that was thoughtless of me. From the viewpoint of the lady next door, it was as if she were suddenly being shown another part—a secret part—of her own child's life which she had been unaware of until now, and right when she was still in the midst of sorrow at having lost this "child." It would not be possible to go through the garden and see Chibi's mother crying. It just wasn't allowed. There's no way we could expect her to share her grief with us.

I attempted to surmise what the neighbor lady's feelings might be in this situation. And I began to think that perhaps my thoughtlessness had been due to my lack of experience in this sort of thing, or maybe even some sort of immaturity on my part.

Several months later, I abruptly submitted an essay (which was to bring the series to a close) that covered the events corresponding to the point in the novel where the cat stopped coming over up to the discovery of her death. Though not well-known, the small magazine was produced by a highly respected publisher and was sold in bookstores oriented toward serious literature.

The reason this very proper lady did not get in touch with me again despite her promises to do so must have been because she was still much too stricken with anger and grief. And her resentment had obviously been directed at me. So when my essays arrived on top of that, it must have made things all the more complicated.

Perhaps the main reason for her anger was the fact that we had been affectionate with Chibi and had become close to the cat without her knowledge and without her permission. But on the other hand, would the mere fact of shared affection lead directly to resentment? If the issue involved permission, then would things have been different if permission had been given? After all, a cat left outside on its own will cross any border it wants.

Or something about the fact of having it all put into print gave the neighbors an estranged or alienating feeling, as if the pet they loved had been abducted by strangers. This must be the root of a kind of secondary resentment.

But a piece of writing, no matter how you interpret it, isn't the same thing as an abduction. The act of writing also crosses borders indiscriminately. Wouldn't there be a way to cleanse that thing looming between the neighbor and myself—to purify boundaries and all by performing an even closer examination of the issue through writing?

We took a look at an apartment in a new high-rise building located about a half a mile to the south, but the windows didn't face the right direction for a view of the zelkova. We just walked home shaking our heads.

As my wife and I walked down Lightning Alley toward our small side gate, a man walked toward us, dressed in casual attire, his hands free of any signs of being on the way back from work such as a briefcase, and from the moment he began approaching us from down the street, I noticed that he held his head stiffly, looking straight forward and never at us, with a dark scowl on his face. And as he grew near, his neck twisted strenuously as his face turned toward us. At the moment he passed his expression grew even more menacing. Once inside the house my wife sighed with relief.

"I just don't understand ... why such intense hatred?" She asked. And then she explained to me that it was the husband of the neighbor, and said that she had never been glared at like that by anyone before in her whole life.

My wife talked about how, when she was in elementary school, her dog would often wander around the neighborhood on its own and was treated affectionately by the neighbors. She felt nothing but gratitude for the fact that the dog would be cared for by the people around her: "Why do they hate us so much for taking care of Chibi?"

"Don't worry about it. We did the right thing."

"We didn't even touch her."

"Who knows, he may have been brooding about something else."

"Like what?"

"Like, maybe he's deeply in debt, and now it's all come due and at an excessively high interest rate, and he can't get back on his feet. So now he's at his wits' end and feels like taking it out on everyone else; that's the kind of expression he had."

Of course, this was all nonsense, and it was nonsense thinking it would make my wife feel any better.

In the bath that night I opened the window to let out the steam. Using the electric pump I added water from the well, and as my skin began to feel smooth and slippery from the hot water I suddenly remembered something from just before Chibi died.

Since in fact she wasn't really my cat, and also because she was always spick-and-span, I had never even thought of giving her a bath. But one night Chibi crept up behind me as I scrubbed away—all doors along the approach to the bath were left open, even the outer door to the area with the packed earthen floor, since the bath was situated so that it was protected from view. So when she came to visit, I made up an absurd little song, which I sang to her as I sat in the bathtub.

> *Chibi—hot spring*
> *Chibi the cat, the bathhouse attendant*
> *Rinse my back*
> *Run away with your little hands*

In the garden, still light at this time of the evening after the passing of the spring equinox, a plump thrush bathed itself in the pond. Soon a small chickadee joined in, splashing around in the water as if imitating the other bird. The two of them kept splashing around for some time, again and again climbing up onto the pond's edge only to jump back in.

20

WHEN THE CAT STOPPED COMING, IT SEEMED AS IF THE garden had changed into something dreary and drab. How much we see through colored glasses, I thought.

Spring soon reached its zenith and gave way to early summer. The various flowers almost seemed to be working in concert: the blooms of one variety would give way to the next as their colors changed from season to season, each time redecorating the garden.

Preceded in death by the old man only three months after they moved to the suburban eldercare facility on the day of the Tanabata Festival of the previous year, the old woman continued to call on occasion. As usual, we were most often left with some kind of task—putting in a large order of *kuzuko* starch at the little cake shop in the old part of town she had always patronized, for instance, or picking up some cold medicine at her regular clinic. Whenever she called she would always remind us—"go ahead and use the big house anytime you want," repeating it like a mantra at the end of each telephone call. She must have felt having the big house at our disposal was compensation for asking us to leave by the end of August because of her situation with the inheritance tax. And we used it to our hearts' content, just as she suggested.

"And go ahead and use the bath too," she would say.

Since a bath had been added on to the guesthouse behind the moon-viewing window, there was nothing at all inconvenient about using our own, but the old woman said, "The bath at the big house is larger. You'll be more comfortable there."

The memory I most associated with the bath of the main house was of something that had occurred during the previous year. Early on a summer afternoon, I heard shouts coming from the main house as I sat alone in my room writing. I rushed to see what was going on. The old woman's shouts were coming from the bath. The old man appeared to have just been getting out of the bath and his body, bright pink like a boiled lobster, was leaning over but remained hanging on the edge of the bathtub. The old woman, wearing old-fashioned Japanese work pantaloons, was doing all she could to support him, but was trapped under his weight and couldn't budge.

I hesitated for a moment, then placed my hand on the old man's naked body to help get him to his room. His skin was surprisingly soft and, considering how lean he was, still firm and healthy. There was no oiliness to it—he could almost have been a young schoolboy. With his eyes wide open, the old man chuckled, but seemed at a loss for words: he no longer had the willpower to move on his own. Then suddenly his body went limp and it was like carrying a dead weight. There seemed to be no way to handle him—I tried getting him on my back and then carrying him like a baby, but he was all arms and legs responding to the pull of gravity, merely slipping farther downward the more

I tried to get a hold on him. In the stance of a sumo wrestler, I tried the *double underarm grip* and managed to get him upright but then became helpless to do more.

This is what they mean when they talk about being between a rock and a hard place. There's no moving forward and it's impossible to turn back. But we can't stay here like this forever, I thought. Then I remembered the gardeners who had just arrived that morning at a neighboring house down the road a bit to the north on Lightning Alley. You could still hear the repetitive sound of garden clippers.

I balanced the old man on the edge of the tub in a seated position and left the old woman to keep him propped up, then with beads of sweat still dripping down my forehead I ran out the side gate and into the alleyway, and from down the road called to the men up in the trees.

Four men in puffed-up workers' trousers and leggings slithered down the tree. Then, leaving their transistor radio behind with the music still blaring, one by one they stepped into the old couple's yard. As soon as they saw what was going on in the bath they knew what to do. With few words exchanged, they laid the old man down on his back, then each one grasped a limb, picked him up, and silently carried him out via the veranda and left him in the bedroom on the west side of the house. Then they returned down the hallway to the entrance and, fixing their cloth work boots back on their feet, left as quickly as they'd come, stepping through the front gate in single file, and in a moment were back up in the trees.

And then the sound of the garden clippers could be heard again wafting across the treetops.

21

A YEAR HAD GONE BY SINCE THEY LEFT THE HOUSE ON the day of the Tanabata Festival, and around the end of May the old woman returned home. This was the time of year when the edge of the pond was crawling with tadpoles sprouting arms and legs, and little black frogs about the size of a bean populated the garden. But the old woman was having difficulty recovering from an operation to remove cataracts and could not see all the leaps and bounds taking place around her. Nor did she seem to notice that Chibi was no longer with us. But she did come over to the guesthouse for a visit, and almost in tears thanked us for taking care of the house and the garden.

She stayed for only two weeks. This was to be her last stay, and she spent a little time each day putting the last of the furniture in order before it was sold off to antique stores. The old woman said she wanted to give us some items as keepsakes—the green ceramic brazier in the Ming style which had been placed out in the garden, the large porcelain vase which had been displayed in an alcove, and the little lantern made of natural stones. The antique store people would be in and out for the next few days and would take everything unless we took them.

All we wanted was the little stone lantern that Chibi often perched herself on top of on the west side of the garden in the shade of some bushes. The shape of the lantern was somewhat humorous—it resembled a stack of three big rice cakes, like the ones you see displayed at New Year's, except that where normally they would be stacked in a pyramid (the smallest on top), in this case the largest went on top with the smaller pieces below.

On a refreshingly clear and sunny day just before the rainy season, a photo session had been arranged. Chairs were set up in the garden where the azaleas were in full bloom. Several photos were taken of the old woman, and then some more with my wife standing by her, posing on the veranda. In one photo, they posed as if they were two young girls frolicking, the old woman grasping both my wife's hands in hers.

Then, on a morning in early June, the old woman returned to the apartment complex for the elderly, never again to set foot in the house, but her tenants were unable to be there to see her off.

As it turned out, on that same day a ceremony was being held at an old temple out in the suburbs north of Tokyo commemorating the second anniversary of Y.'s death, and a special section of seats was reserved for close friends and fellow poets. Meanwhile, news suddenly arrived, only two days before this commemoration, of the death of a highly respected older poet, whose funeral was now to be held on the very same day. I felt torn.

The word "to grieve" or "lament" in Japanese is actually made up of two different kanji characters—"sadness" and "resentment." It seems that here two very separate emotions get tangled up. Whenever a large number of people gather, flustered and confused, around the occasion of a death, a lot of quick decisions are made according to consensus, which is fundamentally suspect. Often, within the limited time available, some decisions are made which one would never have dreamed of. In the case of Y.'s death this was more or less how things proceeded from the night of the wake onward. And now I found myself in the awkward position of having been chosen to officiate at this particular ceremony, or shall we say *forced*, as it was one of those things one simply cannot refuse to do.

Tasks were divided among friends and split between the two services which were to take place. The plan was to first attend the older poet's funeral at a temple in the north end of the city, and then rush out to the suburbs to the other, commemorative ceremony. Because the schedule was so tight, I would have to leave the house before the old woman's planned departure.

So we were seen off, instead. The old woman, who had never seen either one of us in formal attire, was delighted to see my wife in mourning dress, and playfully grabbed onto her sleeve, saying repeatedly, "Oh, you look wonderful dear, just divine."

Then, almost breaking into song, she insisted, "I don't really like being seen off anyway."

Meanwhile we just couldn't seem to find a new apartment. There was simply no comparison with what we had now—everything we looked at was small and cramped, expensive, and drab.

We came to realize just how much the housing market had changed in the last three or four years. On the assumption that land prices could only keep rising, people went on with their lives without ever questioning what was going on around them, and the practice of using real estate as collateral to take out a loan, and then to use the cash for speculative investments, was simply taken for granted. Both real estate values and stock prices continued to rise. The change was evident even in our sleepy little neighborhood. At the counter of the local sushi shop one would often overhear young couples discussing plans to speculate in real estate—they would buy a piece of property and then sell it for a profit within the space of a few years—"flipping," they called it. You could change seats and sit in a different part of the restaurant, and find yet another pair talking about the same thing. That's what the times were like then.

Our search for a new apartment gradually wandered farther and farther from my original plan of looking for something in the vicinity of our old house, moving in an outward spiral from the zelkova tree. Even if we went with the current trend, buying rather than renting on the assumption that that would be more profitable, that would mean we'd have to go even farther out into the suburbs before we could find anything that was even close to being affordable.

With an eager young real estate salesman as our guide, we were led around a suburb about forty minutes outside the city center on the express commuter train, and in the course of viewing a variety of properties, we were given a vicarious peek into the private lives of total strangers—everything from a condominium where a woman who was disturbingly clean lived alone (keeping the place extremely tidy on the assumption that she would be reselling it soon), to the home of a professional baseball player (for all intents and purposes an absent father), overflowing with stuffed animals sent home as souvenirs.

As we went around trying out the various spots on the realtor's list, I found myself seriously wondering at what point the situation would really change. It was like staring hard in a dark room and never quite making things out.

Having failed in his attempts to alter the course of the Arno in order to prevent its flooding, a challenge taken up in cooperation with Leonardo da Vinci, Machiavelli wrote the following poem.

The river's fierce current, its wild
Extremity attained, crushing all manner of things
Wherever it reaches

Making one side high and another low
It carves away the bluffs, altering riverbed and river bottom
Overflowing as if to do battle with Mother Earth

Fortune also is unkind, boldly her long tresses
Disarranged—now here, now there,
One after the other, transform all things

Was the goddess Fortuna going on a rampage? Tossed about by her rough waves, moving from place to place, how were we going to manage to find the right current, the one that would lead us to a new home? In my despair, I decided to approach the problem with a sense of detachment.

22

IN MID-JULY, AS THE SEASONAL RAINS CAME TO AN END, the blue figure of a white-tailed skimmer dragonfly appeared on a large rock beside the pond in a perfect spot to catch the sun. Could it be the offspring of the skimmer who in the summer of the previous year came back again and again to kiss the arc of water produced by the spray from the hose? United in the shape of a distorted heart, the blue-and-yellow male and female had flown from branch to branch among the trees. Could this be their child, now emerged from its pupa?

The male skimmer I'd become friends with had vanished by the end of August. For a while I regretted the disappearance of my winged friend and his wife from the garden, which had now also been left behind by the old man and the old woman. But I felt as if that same skimmer had been brought back to life along with the bright light of summer. Then — between the effacement of death and this birth that was in a sense a kind of rebirth — I found vividly recalled to me those who had left and would never return.

As July too approached its end, I found my eyes wandering toward the large rock extending out over the pond each time I went into the garden under the intense afternoon sun. But there was no sign of the white-tailed skimmer. Then I would clap my hands together lightly as I used to, and from out of nowhere a shadow would nonchalantly fly over this way, ever so slightly rippling the air. If I made an arc of water with the hose, the skimmer would fly around it as if filled with glee and then come in even closer, just the like the one before it.

Skillfully avoiding the spiderwebs which could be found everywhere, he appeared to be living an expansive existence, making use of every corner of the garden even as it lapsed into decline. Suddenly I had a thought: I put down the hose and turned off the water and stretched out my left arm with my index finger pointing up in the air. Then the skimmer took a wide turn, coming back around toward me. He quickly approached, and after first pivoting in yet another direction, came in, aligning himself in the direction my finger pointed and finally alighting there.

I was overjoyed, and held my breath. It's him. It must be him. It had been a long time, though the year had gone by quickly. There, in the deserted garden, so isolated from its surroundings as to produce an almost otherworldly atmosphere, for a brief moment I held on my finger those two great compound eyes and four transparent wings.

The slightest movement of my body sent him back up dancing in midair, but in only a moment he returned and again alighted on my finger. And then there were a few more timeless moments of stillness.

A brown-eared bulbul came down from one of the branches of the zelkova in the neighbor's yard to the east, let out a shrill cry, and then flew off again. Startled, the skimmer flew away and did another round of the garden. But I left my finger pointed up in the air and, keeping as still as I could, waited for a while. The skimmer first set itself down on a spot a couple of yards away, but again returned to my finger.

23

ONE NIGHT WE SLEPT OVER IN THE PARLOR OF THE BIG house. Early in the morning I thought I'd heard someone out on the veranda sharpening a kitchen knife. The harsh rays of the late-summer sun combed through the thick foliage of the zelkova tree and poured into the garden. The sound seemed very close, yet when I looked outside no one was there. I slipped into a pair of wooden clogs and walked in the direction of the sound. It seemed to be coming from the grass growing around the roots of a plum tree near the house.

I stared hard to make out what lay between the blades of grass, and a giant praying mantis turned toward me, a cicada with its wings still unfurled held firmly between its front legs.

I have to say the praying mantis is by far my least favorite of all creatures. The sound I had heard like a whetstone scraping against a knife was the sound of the wings of the dying cicada. Or it could have been the menacing sound of the praying mantis's wings as it carried out its assault on its prey.

With the image of this grisly event seared in my brain I went back to bed, but even as I regained my breath I could still hear the sound. Then my wife, who by now was also awake, asked me what was going on. When I told her what I had just witnessed she jumped up and ran out onto the veranda, grabbing the bamboo futon-beater which had been left there. Then she descended to the stepping stones in the garden in her bare feet and pajamas.

I followed her into the garden, and by the time I had caught up with her she had tossed the praying mantis, separated from its prey, into the azaleas. Then she rested the limp cicada on the palm of her hand. It looked for a moment as if he was finished, but then the cicada began making a sound with its green speckled wings and, at first faltering somewhat, took flight, almost hitting the ground at one point but then recovering and, wings beating rapidly, flew up high over the fence on the west side of the garden.

"I suppose the second human who came along this morning must have seemed like a god to the cicada. The first one was an idiot."

Then she got a surprised look on her face and seemed to be running some thought around and around in her brain.

My wife felt very close to animals, but there was one kind of animal she viscerally disliked—ducks. Perhaps if a cicada were being attacked by a duck the idiot in me would become a god and save it. But if the duck were attacking a praying mantis, or if in the unlikely event a praying mantis were throttling a duck, I suppose the two of us would just stay in bed shaking until the whole thing was over.

Funny, these aversions we have for certain things. It does make you wonder a bit whether it's some kind of karmic connection with a past-life experience, even if that's just a bit too weird.

In any case, let us simply assume that, having gotten through this crisis, the cicada was able to live out the rest of its short life to the fullest. And as for the praying mantis, well, I don't really want to think about the praying mantis.

Around this time we at last found a new place to live. At some point we had gotten into the habit of sleeping in the large parlor of the main house, which would most likely soon be sold and then demolished. We were now getting our last taste of the place as our lives fell into a disarray of cardboard boxes in preparation for the move.

24

IT WAS THE LAST SATURDAY OF AUGUST AND THE NIGHT before our scheduled move.

At some point, without our having noticed, the gap left open at the foot of the wooden fence which formed the border between our house and the neighbors to the east, and which in the past had only been partially covered in wire mesh, was completely repaired: a new sheet of wire mesh now covered the entire opening. Meanwhile, it seemed as though some creature had wandered out of the house next door into the area between it and the wire mesh. It seems it was a kitten.

For the first time in quite a while I heard the neighbor woman's voice. I took a rest from packing and strained my ears to listen.

"Look, they're like jewels."

"Uh-huh."

The cat was apparently below the eaves close to the house in the backyard which was also near the little passageway through the border. But there was nothing to worry about. The cat would not go next door. This was more or less the gist of the conversation between mother and child. The cat's eyes must have been glowing in the growing darkness.

"She has such pretty eyes, don't you think?"

Apparently she was looking out from the entry of the house. I could hear the voice of the little boy next to her. From the window on the south side of the house I could see the light from a flashlight move this way and that.

There was really nothing to be bitter about, but it did make me think of Chibi. So they've got a new cat.... My wife also noticed, and seemed a bit uneasy.

The room had reached the pinnacle of chaos. We had to finish packing that night, but no matter how much we worked at it, seemingly out of nowhere objects continued to appear. We had to call the movers more than once as work progressed during the day to order more boxes—in the end we needed over a hundred. Most of it was books we just couldn't part with and bric-a-brac collected over the years. The endless job of packing so exhausted me that I almost burst into something between a scream and insane laughter. But then something began to push me in the opposite direction.

For my wife, mainly it was sad that a certain someone once cared for by her family would now be forgotten at the foot of the little pine tree. But not only that, just by moving away, we also would be joining sides with those who forget—this was simply unbearable.

Finding a new cat would be the quickest and most effective means of soothing the sadness. This was the accepted wisdom. And it appeared that the neighbors had resorted to that approach. So they had carefully, even rigorously repaired the wire mesh covering the gap left open in the boundary dividing their yard from the outside so that past events would not be repeated. Then they went out and got a new cat.

We also began to drop by the local pet shops in passing to take a little peek through the shop windows. But each time we did this my wife just shook her head. No matter how cute and lovable the cats might be it just wasn't the same.

This was an indication of that essential something which still connected her to Chibi like an invisible thread.

Then one day as we rode our bikes, one behind the other, to a distant neighborhood, we stumbled upon several kittens which appeared to belong to someone on a little side street we had never ventured down before. My wife was stopped in her tracks and got off of her bike to have a closer look at the little fuzzy creatures.

"Shall I go talk to the people here to see if we can have one?"

I asked the question with emphasis. She thought for a while and then said, "No, it's just not the same."

She laughed sadly and stood up to leave.

We stacked the cardboard boxes we had stuffed with all our belongings in the spacious parlor of the big house, but no sooner had we done so than the guesthouse again was filled with boxes.

One box remained untouched in a corner of the tatami room, its cover left open. A towel was laid at the bottom of the box and a dish, smelling of horse mackerel, was set down there along with it.

25

WHAT WE FINALLY FOUND WAS A LOW-RISE CONDOMIN-
ium set back in a grove of zelkova trees.

We had searched far and wide, even going out to the farthest
western reaches of the city, then, empty-handed, we'd found
ourselves turning back and starting all over again near our own
neighborhood. It was the middle of July, and our deadline was
the end of August. So we mounted our bicycles and went around
to every realtor we could find in the area. Then suddenly I was
reminded of how we had found the old woman's guesthouse four
years before. So we again dropped in at the realtor just outside
the local train station and my wife immediately laid her eyes on
a property whose information had just recently been pasted up
on the bulletin board. We asked about it and were told it was on
the third floor of a rental condominium in a setting that was like
being out in the woods.

We pedaled out to see it right away on our bicycles. It was an
apartment building with three floors containing forty units. Next
to it was an open space planted with trees which were preserved
by the local district government. There was a row of about twenty
huge zelkova trees, and to the east there was a neighborhood

consisting of old traditional houses. It was midway between two local stations and near a railroad crossing, probably the reason the natural wooded area had been preserved. We were told that there had been a golf driving range there up until a few years previous to our discovering it. The rent was double what we'd been paying at our old place and we would require a guarantor who could vouch for our income, and of course no pets were allowed.

We had searched for a way to buy a place, but each time found ourselves lamenting our financial situation which almost got us there but not quite. And to top it off, it seems that we were always shown places that were considerably run down. But soon we realized this had become the norm. I recalled that the last time we looked for a new apartment, as well as the time before that, things just hadn't been like this in the city. Even in our neighborhood, we started to notice a growing number of older houses being readied for demolition so that shiny new condominiums could be built in their place.

Having seen more than our share of dumps we were not exactly in a position to turn up our noses at an apartment complex enveloped in greenery. And only a seven-minute walk would find us at Chibi's zelkova. And who knew, maybe the rustling of the leaves of the zelkova trees outside our window would bring us visions of Chibi's own tree.

It was early August and several days had passed since shelling out the deposit. I decided to take a walk alone and found myself wandering toward the place where we would soon be living.

Entering the property I looked up at the dense foliage and the green of the zelkova trees, leaves rustling in the light breeze. On the south side of the L-shaped building was a greenbelt closed off with a fence and a gate so that one normally could not enter. The apartment we would be renting was located on the third floor, accessed via a staircase set into the right angle of the L shape. A family was still living there. As I strained my neck to look up at the window facing north, I could hear their excited chatter—all about how they would be moving to their own house soon, a real house.

Circling around the building to the right there was an empty lot that had not yet been cleared for new construction. I walked onto the uneven surface of the lot when suddenly there among the weeds appeared a skinny mother cat with four kittens suckling at her belly. Startled by the sound of footsteps, the four kittens, which could not have been more than a month old, sprang from their mother's teats and scattered, then, stopping where they were, looked back at me. Meanwhile the mother cat, though maintaining a healthy suspicion, remained just where she was, striking an attitude of majestic composure. The entire right side of her face was white, while the left was black, producing a unique pattern. Her kittens, who stood transfixed around her, were each a variation on the theme, but all in all were the kind of cats one tended to see around quite often—the spotted variety if you will, whose fur was white with round or nearly round splotches the color of India ink.

Not wanting to ruin their meal, I turned on my heel and retreated.

We moved at the end of August. The old woman's house was to have gone on sale soon after that, but apparently they could not find a buyer immediately due to disagreements on the terms.

Somehow it seemed as if a major collapse was on its way.

I called the old woman at her new home in the suburbs to tell her we had moved just a ten-minute walk away from the old house and she seemed delighted.

"Could you drop by and check on things from time to time? I'd feel a lot more comfortable if you would."

So I took the key and went inside the abandoned garden. I stood there alone for a while. The old man and the old woman were gone. My wife and the cat also were no longer there, and I too was already gone.

26

THE FOUR KITTENS FLITTED AROUND THE SHRUBBERY and in addition to the black-and-white mother cat, there was a father cat with dark gray fur. Unusual to see in stray cats, but the whole intact family inhabited the area.

When autumn came the mother cat could no longer be found, and the shadows of leaps and bounds seemed also to have declined in the bushes from the original four to only three kittens. One of them looked a bit like Chibi, with the same pattern of spots on its fur. We began to call the little group of three cats "The Chibi-Chibis."

The three kittens and their father were always loitering around the entrance of the building. To be precise, one of the kittens (always the same one) would position herself between the planters in a location where she would not get in the way of people entering or leaving—she would sit there politely, paws tucked in front. The remaining three, including the father cat, would stay hidden in the shadow of the azaleas.

How their roles had been decided I did not know, but it seems the idea was for the best-looking of the kittens to attract the residents' attention. Thinking she was cute, they would leave scraps near the concrete border of one of the planters. Then the other three cats would emerge from behind to take the scraps. The pretty kitten didn't take any for herself. Only after the others had eaten and settled down would she have her own meal. We called the prettiest member of the three Chibi-Chibis "Big Sister" while the toughest we named "Shiro" for his almost completely white fur, and the clumsiest of the three we called "Kappa," since his tortoiseshell markings reminded us of the river spirits of traditional folklore.

The father cat, always calm and serious, we simply called "Papa."

There was no doubt that Big Sister looked like Chibi. But no matter how hard you looked—on earth or in heaven—there was no cat as otherworldly and mysterious as Chibi. In contrast, Big Sister had a down-to-earth quality as well as a soft and tranquil nature. She was shaped a bit like a pear and had a short tail. It was almost as if she had been pulled out of an animated film—and that gave her a certain attraction.

Arriving back home my wife would announce the group's activities.

"Big Sister's out there again."

"She's a cutie, isn't she."

"I'll go bring her a little something."

It seemed almost like old times, when Chibi would come over to our house and we would play in the garden. Soon autumn deepened and feeding the cats had become our daily routine.

There were other residents who were fond of the cats and left scraps, but for my wife it was on a whole different level. One night she announced, "I'm going outside to play with the cats."

She took out some dried sardines and then got the Ping-Pong

ball out of Chibi's old box in the closet. But then after a while she came back despondent.

"She won't play. Even when I put the ball right in front of her, she won't try batting it once. She doesn't seem to understand the concept of play."

And she got that look on her face again, the one she got when she was thinking of Chibi.

Then, around the time the autumn leaves began to blow around the apartment's grounds, Big Sister started to play. The family of strays became accustomed to getting a late-night snack, and then in the wee hours when none of the other residents were around to see, my wife would go out to play with Big Sister. The Ping-Pong ball didn't bounce well on the asphalt surface of the road, so we tied a piece of string to the end of a stick, and on the other end of the string tied a little snowman doll. My wife would pull and shake the string and play all around the entrance of the building with Big Sister. The other cats just watched from the safety of the shrubs. In the midst of play, Big Sister would suddenly crouch and shake her head vigorously, then cough a really bad-sounding cough. The whole time her coughing echoed through the entrance both my wife and the other cats looked on with worried expressions.

One night in mid-February, Big Sister followed the snowman doll all the way up to the dreaded third floor of the building. From the crack in the metal door she peered inside to see what was there. We didn't want to force her to come in, so we just propped the door open with a sandal and left it up to her to do whatever she wanted to do.

Quietly, and gingerly, she tiptoed around the room, taking in each detail of her first inside view of a human house. Then our guest like others before her slipped back through the door without a word and quickly descended the stairs to return to her outdoor family.

My wife followed her outside and down the stairs to the building's entry. Crouching low on the ground the gray father cat was waiting for her. In front of my wife's very eyes, he batted Big Sister on the head once with his paw. Big Sister shut her eyes and let out a small cry.

The next day we went on a trip, leaving the apartment empty for a week. It was to attend a relative's wedding in Kyushu, where we both grew up, so we decided to make it a homecoming visit and take time to see our families. My wife's hometown was in the same province as mine, and on the way back she stopped to visit her folks and I took the night train home by myself.

The entry to the apartment complex had a roadway for cars to enter on one side and a pedestrian entrance on the other. The cat family tended to stay within earshot of the entryway in the shrubs on the side of the road, but would never venture inside the brightly lit hall where the mailboxes were located.

As I turned the corner where the landlord lived and approached the building, I wondered whether the cats had managed to get enough to eat while we were gone. The night's darkness increased as I walked beneath the thick foliage of the zelkova trees, but then I saw the bright light of the entryway float up before me. It was the only well-lit spot on the grounds of the building. As I walked up to the door a small white form bounded out of the darkness and into the fluorescent light, running toward me and meowing all the way.

27

BIG SISTER BEGAN COMING UPSTAIRS TO THE THIRD floor on her own, whenever she wanted to. Every once in a while she would shake her head back and forth like a papier-mâché doll and let out a series of bad-sounding coughs. We worried about how she would get through the cold weather in this shape.

We always propped open the door with a sandal so she could leave whenever she wanted, but a couple of days into the New Year's holiday we began closing it. We bought a plastic box and filled it with cat litter. It was our first official shopping expedition for the New Year. Then my wife suggested, "Why don't we bring Kappa up too."

He always lagged behind the other members of the family, and he was timid and unsteady on his feet: Kappa seemed the least capable of surviving outdoors. My wife appeared to be moving in the direction of adopting the whole family, but keeping even one for the night, constantly meowing because she wasn't used to staying inside with humans, was already causing enough of a problem. And since pets were not allowed in the building that also meant that we would have to be prepared for the possibility of getting kicked out.

And on top of that, Kappa did not look like he was anywhere near prepared to climb the stairs to the third floor on his own. He didn't even show any signs of responding to the snowman doll when it was dangled before him in the bushes. Bringing him upstairs would necessitate devising a clever new strategy.

We had never kept a skylark or any other kind of bird for a pet, but for whatever reason, we owned a birdcage especially made for a skylark. It was an old piece of bamboo workmanship shaped something like an elongated cylinder, so that it stood quite tall when placed vertically, as originally designed. I suggested fixing the door of the cage with a device which would cause it to close, trapping whatever creature might enter inside, and placing the cage in the empty lot in the middle of the night with some food to act as bait, and then waiting in the shadows for the cat to come. As it turned out, the person who proposed this strategy (yours truly) ended up being the one to carry it out.

On a cold night during the first week of the New Year, Kappa approached the birdcage. He circled the cage a few times examining it, before quietly stepping in through the open door, but then something unexpected happened in the mind of the would-be captor. Somehow I couldn't bring myself to pull the string. If I were to close the cage door now, Kappa would be frightened and upset, and probably put up a violent struggle. Then the cage would fall over and roll around on the ground, becoming an even more frightening place to be stuck in, and then how could Kappa truly become ours, having come to us through such a traumatic experience? All I had to do now was to pull the string and the cage door would come down, but I couldn't do it.

Kappa cautiously ate the food and in his usual clumsy way turned around inside the cage. Then he gazed in my direction with those round eyes giving no hint of any suspicions, and stepping through the dreaded entrance, he looked at me again. After a slow start, he moved into a gallop, bounded across the pavement under the bare zelkova trees, and ran off the property.

Gazing intently at the sleeping cat on the same sofa where Chibi used to sleep, wearing a collar quite similar to Chibi's with comma-shaped beads, my wife sighed, "She's mine."

Yet despite her satisfaction, it looked like it was going to be a while before it would be possible to hold the cat and pet her. And we would have to take her to the vet soon for shots and whatnot. But in any case, we decided that we should first give her a proper name.

28

SINCE THE MID-1980S, STOCK PRICES AND REAL ESTATE had continued to skyrocket, but by the first half of 1990 things began to collapse. It was the beginning of autumn when I heard that the old woman had put the house up for sale. Already the economy was showing signs of slipping.

By 1991 the reality of the situation had become obvious—the bloated economy had completely collapsed, throwing the entire country into confusion. Then August came. As I sat half-heartedly watching television, a commercial for a major homebuilder came on. I could hear the eerily calm voice of the narrator saying, "What a father passes on to his children …"

And then … "Building homes is like raising children."

In front of a house with a traditional gate shaded by the branch of a pine tree, a father places his hand on the head of a very young boy. The two bow politely to passersby and exchange greetings with a smile. The scene was shown in black and white. Somehow the wooden fence, which could be seen behind them, looked familiar to me.

I took a walk to double-check, and I could tell that the commercial definitely featured the house where we once lived by the pattern of stains on the mud wall and the way the bamboo slats were laid.

You could see right through the commercial: obviously the housing industry was trying to make a sudden change of direction from its recent tendency of encouraging people to sell older houses like this one and buy new ones so they could take advantage of the skyrocketing real estate prices. The old house was merely a prop to give the real estate company a clean image, while in actual fact it sat there silently awaiting demolition.

So, late that summer, using the passkey which I still had in my possession, I went inside for a last look. The garden was smothered in tall weeds and the pond was all dried up. There was no sign of its former charm or of all the animal life which used to fill it. What happened to the dragonflies? And the praying mantis? Now overgrown, the Japanese holly and the azaleas had lost their perfectly pruned round shapes and were deflated into oddly distorted hemispheres. Only the Rose of Sharon winding its way up the wall of the toolshed was in bloom, swaying in the soft light of summer's end.

In December of 1991 we visited the old woman at her condominium in the suburbs out west of the city. During three hours of pleasant chat the subject of real estate was barely touched upon. As it turned out, she'd been forced to sell the house at a price much lower than she had originally hoped. Finally it had been split into three parcels and sold. Demolition was set to begin in the middle of January in the coming year.

A few days later she asked us to go check on how things were going at the house. A section of the fence lining the alley had collapsed. It was leaning over into the garden: I just propped it back up as a stopgap measure, nothing you could really call a repair.

Three days into the new year the last few odds and ends at the old house were being cleaned up, so we decided to drop by once more and transplant to a pot some of the Reeves Spirea they had let us plant in the garden and take it home with us. When we arrived we discovered that the keyhole had been plugged and there was no way for us to open the front gate. So my wife slipped through a little space left open in the fence when I'd propped it up and let me in through the side gate.

The boundless growth of wild grass which covered the garden in summer had dried up and now it was in every sense abandoned. Metal markers that looked like spikes had been driven into the ground midway across the garden. You could tell how they were dividing up the land from these markers. The trees were all drastically cut back, and my eyes were pierced by the plum branches, the only ones sprouting buds.

Looking up at the clear blue wintry sky, you could see the bare branches of the zelkova tree swaying in the breeze, its bark sparkling like oxidized metal.

While my wife dug up the Reeves spirea, I rolled up the rattan matt we had left in the middle of the hardwood floor of the guesthouse and tied a string around it. I remembered vividly the daily arrival of our guest through the floor-level window, so much so that I could even point out exactly where she had first set foot.

On the sixteenth of January I went back again. Scaffolding had been set up around the house and orange tarps had been hung all along the fence, covering the entire property. There would be no more images forming of people passing along the alleyway through the knothole in the fence. The demolition was to be carried out over the next five days.

On the last day of January it rained all afternoon and by evening it had turned to snow. The snow fell silently and steadily. I had shut myself away all day working, so for a change of pace I went out with my wife into the white night and on to the local shopping district. After a bite to eat we found ourselves walking in the direction of the old house. The snow was falling thick now and our feet made a crunching sound as we trudged along through the cold night air.

We passed wordlessly by the house with the Japanese plume grass, then descended the slope until there on the left, where the old mansion used to be, was a huge vacant lot. The neighbor's house and Lightning Alley were now completely exposed to view from the main thoroughfare. The snow continued to fall.

There it lay in the darkness—a raw, open space covered by a sheet of pure white.

A WRITER ACQUAINTANCE, WHOM WE SHALL REFER TO
simply as H., lived just a minute's walk down Lightning Alley toward the south end. I had never had the occasion to visit before,
but we had begun a collaboration, so now we would often take
the same train home.

H. had moved to the area with his family in 1950 when he
was only five years old, and he could remember a time when
there were still farms in the area. A creek used to cut across
the fields just before the slope and it would flood whenever
it rained heavily.

When I asked him about the alleyway he let out a chuckle
and said, "It's kind of a strange place, isn't it. For years and
years there was always such an interesting collection of people living there, right on that one little street—a sculptor and
printmaker, a zoologist, a geologist, a musician, and a photographer of Buddhist statuary."

And then H. told me something quite unexpected—apparently the family who had once been Chibi's owners had
moved to the suburbs, to a magnificent house sitting in the
shade of a huge zelkova tree. I had thought that they would

always remain there, but apparently they had their reasons—the children's schooling or something like that. But in any case, it seemed as if Chibi had been left all alone.

I remember it was the night of the full moon on the eleventh of March when Chibi died. Since then, every year on that date, late in the night, I walk with my wife to the spot where she was last found lying on the ground in front of the house with the Japanese plume grass just before the entryway. We choose an hour when there are few passersby, and when the time is right, we place a few dried sardines on the ground, then kneel down and place our hands together. Then we take a leisurely walk down to our former abode.

I have come to realize that during this entire ten years, each time I have joined my hands together there I have never been able to believe even once that she was hit by a car. I haven't spoken to my wife about this.

It was always a quiet street. Whether we're talking about a car which has just crossed the street where most of the traffic is and turned onto this road heading downhill, or one which is headed up the hill and has reached the intersection, this is right at the point where drivers are forced to slow down. So whenever I have visited this spot and crouched down on the ground, placing my hands together in prayer with my back to the passing cars, I have always thought Chibi would have been able to dodge a car with no problem.

And there's another thing I've just noticed as I reshape this loose collection of essays and journal notes into a novel. The eleventh of March fell on a Sunday that year. It had been the evening of Saturday, the tenth, when we'd gone to the "Lightning Catcher" exhibit. We returned home a little after ten that night and found that the cat food in the dish placed in the box in the corner of the Japanese tatami room had decreased somewhat. On Sunday, the eleventh, there were no signs that Chibi had touched the horse mackerel or had disturbed the cotton cloth covering the floor-level window through which she would enter the house.

According to the notes I took down in my pocket memo book, it was after eleven thirty on the night of the eleventh that the woman found her lying on the ground, *not* the tenth according to her story. Just shortly before then, around eleven, Chibi had apparently been asleep with her family, this also according to the neighbor's explanation.

How events unfold depends on an infinite number of mundane factors that are interconnected by virtue of their order of occurrence, and without which said event could not have occurred. But memory is less precise. Just before leaving for the exhibit I saw Chibi, her back turned to me. It was the last time I would see her. And because of this I had always mistakenly assumed that it was eleven thirty on the tenth when she was found lying in the street. And then, based on that, I went on to make another mistaken assumption—that the reason we set the anniversary of her death on March 11th was because by that morning she would have been unmistakably dead—cold and stiff.

I suppose I was so disturbed by the reality of death I was somehow not seeing the essentials. As I approached the final phase of this book, I found myself going back over the events as they unfolded, and finally became aware of this point.

What this means is that between the hours of 10 P.M. on March 10th and 11 P.M. on March 11th, Chibi was safe, and yet she did not come see us. She used to come over so frequently ... she came every day—and even if she were hurt—she would come over to show us where she was hurt—and yet even though she was safe, on that one day alone she did not come. How could that be? And yet that is indeed the truth.

So in other words, Chibi spent the last day of her life in a wholly different way than she ever had before. All I want is to know what happened—I want to somehow grasp every detail of the events of that day, that one day like a tiny dewdrop ... but now it's all engulfed in the profound darkness of time.

"I never go that way on my own."

The words of the neighbor woman, speaking of the house with the Japanese plume grass, now stick in my mind and I have them written down here in my book.

Translator's Notes

Chapter 2: The Shōwa Period in Japanese history lasted from 1926 to 1989—the reign of Emperor Hirohito. Its end at the Emperor's death was felt to be symbolic on a number of levels.

Chapter 4: Hiraide's text actually refers to the early Shōwa Period (1926–31), which was a time of great creativity and freedom, especially of major Modernist literary and artistic output.

Up until the 1930s a military officer would still have been a cultured gentleman—a great contrast with later years.

"The direction of fire" refers to Japan's traditional calendar, based on the Chinese Zodiac. The calendar is made up of the Yin and Yang aspects of the five elements. The third sign is Fire (Yang). The character is 丙. The direction associated with this calendar sign is south by southeast.

Chapter 5: In older, traditional houses and apartments, room sizes were based on the number of tatami mats used. Two tatami mats is approximately 35 sq. ft. The six tatami mat room would be just a bit more than 116 square feet.

A tokonoma is a traditional raised alcove used to display flower arrangements or fine ceramics. The wall of the alcove would usually have a hanging scroll with calligraphy and perhaps a traditional ink painting. This is not the decor of an average apartment. Nowadays this would be considered quite luxurious.

Chapter 6: The northern suburb is Saitama Prefecture.

Chapter 7: As Emperor Hirohito lay on his deathbed in late 1988, the government asked the populace to refrain from festive or frivolous activities such as going out and drinking or dancing, etc. It was decided that it would be most proper for the entire nation to act in a somber manner out of respect for the emperor. Though there were protests from businesses such as restaurants and bars, and of course the Socialist and Communist parties flew into a rage, most citizens actually behaved with the suggested "restraint." Hiraide's sentence has a certain tongue-in-cheek quality, referring to this activity as if it were the latest fad.

About Mrs. Muddy: The name in Japanese, "Doro," means mud, but is also the beginning of the word "dorobou," which means burglar or thief.

The New Year is Japan's most important holiday. Most employers give their employees the entire week off and people spend time visiting family. Although keeping to his desk to a large degree, Hiraide does manage to get in the minimum activities—a visit to a Buddhist temple to ring the temple bell (the bell is rung a total of 108 times to ring in the New Year: visitors get one shot each), then a visit to a Shinto shrine and a traditional new year's treat of buckwheat noodles (soba).

"The emperor finally succumbed": Hiraide uses a special term here, used in respect, for the death of a king. There is a whole specialized vocabulary associated with the Japanese emperor.

Chapter 10: The Tanabata Festival, or star festival (which originated in China), is celebrated on July 7 when the stars Vega and Altair meet.

Chapter 11: "1989, a year in which we entered a new era with its own name." Each imperial period designates the reign of a particular emperor and has the name of that emperor. The current era, which started in 1989, is Heisei (which, ironically enough, literally means "normal and uneventful"). Use of the imperial era date seems to be falling out of practice except for on government documents.

Chapter 15: In Japan's classics, the *Nihon Shoki* is the second oldest work. Compiled in the 8th century, it begins with the creation myth, and includes songs and oral tales of the gods. Unlike Japan's other mythical text, the Kojiki, it includes the first few emperors. It is generally agreed by scholars that the purpose of collecting the tales was to bring legitimacy to the Yamato clan's rule in ancient Nara. The text was written in Chinese characters (kanji), which had only recently been introduced in Japan. At that time kanji were used for their sound values in an attempt to represent sounds in the Japanese language, though some characters were also used for their meanings. The classical language and its imperfect expression in 8th-century Chinese characters is highly complex and understood only by scholars. Hiraide appears to have used a modern translation which retains a classical air.

Regarding the two possible readings of "Lightning Catcher": what can be difficult for the English-speaking reader to understand is just what would be unusual about assuming that the name lightning catcher should be focused on the subject (i.e. one who catches lightning). This stems from the difference between a western language in which subject and object are clearly separated, and in which the subject is always, obviously "I" (an accident of grammar according to Wittgenstein), and a language like Japanese in which the subject is most often absent, and where subject-object confusion or even complete merging is the norm.

Chapter 19: In Japan, well known as a society of insiders and outsiders, the ultimate insider is of course a member of the family—a blood relation, and anything else associated with the family unit, including cats. So the bohemian writer couple has inadvertently trespassed on the sanctity of the Confucian family structure by virtue of maintaining a "secret" relationship with the neighbor's cat. These missteps lead to the narrator's musings on writing as well as on the philosophical implications of the boundary between the narrator and the neighbor (i.e., self and other).